TWILIGHT OF EMBERS

DRAGONS OF EMBER HOLLOW

TESSA HALE

Cover Design: Hang Le
Paperback Formatting: Champagne Book Design

TWILIGHT
OF
EMBERS

PROLOGUE

Hayden
PAST, AGE ELEVEN

THE FLASHLIGHT BEAM SHIFTED AGAINST MY makeshift tent, and I reached out to adjust it, pulling the blankets higher over my head. Any glimmer of light from under my door, and my parents would be in here in seconds to confiscate my book.

I rolled my lips over my teeth as I glanced at my watch. Eleven-forty-three. I'd turn out the light at midnight. But, for now, Nancy Drew had a mystery to solve, and we were just getting to the good part.

Voices sounded from downstairs, and I frowned. My parents were night owls, but they were usually quiet as mice. The only way I knew they stayed up was that I'd been caught reading more times than I could count.

Footsteps pounded on the stairs, and my eyebrows pulled together. What the heck was going on?

My bedroom door was wrenched open. "Hayden!"

My mom's single word was part whisper, part yell. I threw the covers off myself, and my flashlight tumbled to the mattress.

"Mom?"

Her violet eyes looked wild as the light from the hallway hit them. The same violet eyes that she'd given to me. She grabbed my hand and tugged me out of bed. "Hurry."

"What's going on?"

My father shouted something from downstairs in a language I didn't recognize, and Mom's face went pale. We shared our fair complexion, but this was a sickly hue. One I'd only seen the time she'd accidentally sliced her finger while cutting carrots. She'd never liked the sight of blood.

Mom tugged me into the hallway and toward their bedroom.

"Mom?" I croaked.

She pulled me into their small closet and tugged a cedar chest into the middle of the space. Climbing on top of the chest, she pushed on a panel in the ceiling. I blinked a few times. I didn't even know there was an attic in this house, let alone a door in the ceiling.

My mom's gaze locked with mine, and her eyes shimmered with unshed tears. "I'm going to lift you up, and you'll shut the door behind you. Don't move, and don't make a sound. Whatever you hear, don't come out."

My own eyes filled with tears. "What's happening?"

She hauled me up onto the chest and hugged me tight. "I love you more than you'll ever know. You're my miracle."

My tears came faster. "Mom—"

A bang sounded downstairs, and my mom jerked.

"Up. Now," she ordered as she lifted.

My mom had always been strong, but tonight, it was as if I weighed no more than a feather. I grabbed hold of the opening and hoisted myself up. "You come, too," I told her.

She shook her head, blonde hair cascading around her shoulders. "I need to help your dad. Remember, don't come out no matter what you hear. Not until the police are here. Listen for the sirens."

My tears fell, one landing on my mom's cheek, but she didn't move to wipe it away. "Don't leave me."

Pain streaked across her face. "Never. I'm always with you. Always here." She placed a hand over her heart.

Another noise came from downstairs, one that almost sounded like an explosion.

Mom jumped down from the chest, shoving it back against the wall. "Close the door, Hayden."

I didn't move for a moment. Couldn't.

"Please," she begged.

It was the desperation in her voice that had me moving. I hefted the door closed. But just before it latched, I heard her whisper, "Love you forever."

The darkness swirled around me, choking. As if its tendrils were reaching right into my throat. Why hadn't I grabbed my flashlight? Anything to fight it off.

Muffled shouts sounded, and then my mother yelled. A deeper voice snarled something in a language I didn't recognize. There was a crackle and a bang.

I jumped, then tried to grip the rough wood floor. Splinters dug into my palms, but the pain was a welcome distraction.

My heart thudded against my ribs. The beat of it radiated through my body, the pulse so loud it was deafening.

"*Càit a bheil a' bhana-phrionnsa?*" the deep voice snarled.

My mom snapped something back in that same unfamiliar language. I'd never heard it before. Not once. How was it possible that my parents spoke an entirely different language and I didn't know it?

"*Bana-phrionnsa!*" the man yelled. The force of his voice was so loud I swore it made the walls shake. "Where *is* she?"

"You'll never have her," my mom screamed back.

There was silence for a moment and then a scream. My mother's scream.

My fingers flew to the latch on the door as my mom's words filled my head. "*Whatever you hear, don't come out.*"

But she'd screamed. It sounded like one of pain. I had to help.

The man spoke in that same rapid-fire language. Another deep voice spoke back, but I didn't hear my mother's voice at all, my father's either.

Sirens sounded in the distance, and a muttered curse filled the air. It was quickly followed by heavy footsteps.

"I checked all the bedrooms. The closets. The basement. She's nowhere," a younger voice said.

"A little girl doesn't just disappear," the man snarled.

"They might have had her run," the younger voice replied. "We need to move. The cops are coming."

"I want the woods searched. I won't let her slip through my fingers. Not again."

"Yes, alpha," the younger voice said.

There were footsteps again as the sirens grew steadily louder, but no more noise came from within the room. My fingers tightened around the door latch. I couldn't wait a second longer. I hauled it open and peered out.

Light streamed in from my parents' bedroom, but I couldn't make out anything other than the closet.

Scooting to the edge of the opening, I gripped the side and let myself slide out. Hanging from the attic space, I glanced down. It was only about a three-foot drop. I just hoped those men weren't present to hear it.

I released my hold.

My bare feet hit the carpet, and I landed with an oomph. The second I did, my head lifted, and I pushed to my feet. But I didn't make it more than three steps before I froze.

"No." I didn't recognize the voice, even though I felt it come from me. It was strangled, inhuman.

My feet propelled me forward, but I fell to my knees. Into a pool of blood. It wasn't bright red like in the movies. It was deeper. Almost closer to brown. And it spilled out of my mother, surrounding her.

Her violet eyes were open, unblinking.

"Mom," I croaked, my hands hovering over her. What did I do? How did I help?

There was a hole in her chest. Right over where her heart should've been.

I placed my hands over it as if I could somehow will the blood she needed back into her body. As if I could save her.

But I couldn't. And I couldn't save myself either.

CHAPTER ONE

Hayden
PRESENT, AGE NINETEEN

THE COACH BUS JOLTED AS IT HIT A POTHOLE. I grabbed hold of the armrest, and the older woman next to me gave me a kind smile. The dark skin crinkled around her eyes as she did, telling me she made the action often.

I was used to looking for those kinds of signs—whether someone frowned or smiled often. It was a sort of early detection system, and it had saved my butt more times than I could count.

The woman lowered her knitting project. "These roads certainly aren't for the faint of heart."

I grimaced but let out a chuckle. "I'm glad I didn't eat a heavy breakfast, that's for sure."

We'd been winding around mountain roads through Northern California for the past hour. Roads that hadn't been especially well preserved.

The woman laughed. "My son is lucky I love him enough to make this trip to visit."

My heart ached at that. It didn't matter how many years had

passed since I'd lost my own parents; I still got that horrible suck-ing pain when I was reminded of all I was missing. I'd been lucky to land with a good foster family on the third placement. A foster family who'd kept me all these years and let me stay with them even after I turned eighteen so that I could finish high school.

But even with that strike of luck and their kindness in the face of my tragedy, it wasn't the same as the love of my own parents. It was always just a bit stilted, awkward. Like staying in a hotel for eight years instead of your own home.

"That's nice. Where does he live?" I asked, forcing a smile.

The woman picked up her knitting again, her fingers moving the yarn deftly. "In Hamilton—just a few more stops. Where are you headed?"

"Ember Hollow. I'm starting at Evergreen University."

It still felt unreal. After struggling for the first year after my parents' deaths, I'd found my stride academically. I'd managed to get a full ride to the small, private university nestled in the redwoods.

My seatmate let out a low whistle. "Must be a smart cookie."

"I'm okay, but I know how to study hard." School had given me somewhere to lose myself. I couldn't drown in grief if I was too focused on calculus equations or anatomy.

"Work ethic is more important than ability any day."

"I hope you're right," I said with a smile. I was determined to do well here. To make all I could of the pre-med track so that I could secure another full ride to medical school.

As the bus rounded a curve, a zap of energy coursed through me. It was like static electricity on steroids or maybe being hit by lightning.

"Are you okay?" the woman next to me asked. "You went a little pale."

I shook it off as a sign reading *Welcome to Ember Hollow, Population 2013* came into view.

"I guess I have those new-school jitters."

She gave me another of her warm smiles. "You'll do great, honey. Don't you fret."

The bus jerked as it turned, and the driver reached overhead for his microphone. "Approaching Ember Hollow. First stop, Evergreen University."

"Thanks for the vote of confidence."

I peered out the window as the thick forest gave way to a picturesque downtown. It had an Old West vibe, a complete one-eighty from the Seattle suburb I'd lived in for the past eight years. There were antique lampposts and even old hitching posts. I couldn't help but wonder if people still rode horses into town.

The bus turned again, away from downtown and onto campus. The sign for Evergreen University was carved into stone. It looked fancy, and a feeling of unease trickled over me.

I'd worked hard at my after-school job for the past three years. I'd saved up so that I'd have some extra spending money for college. But I certainly wasn't rolling in it.

The bus slowed, making a hissing sound as it came to a stop.

"Everyone for Ember Hollow, Evergreen University."

I stood and grabbed my backpack as the older woman rose to allow me out.

"You knock 'em dead, honey."

I grinned at her. "I'll give it my best shot."

Slinging my backpack over my shoulder, I grabbed my duffel from the overhead compartment and made my way down the aisle. Two other passengers got off before me and made their way to where the driver was by the luggage bays.

I started toward campus before the driver called out.

"Don't you have a suitcase?"

I turned, shaking my head. "I've got everything here."

I didn't have much to bring with me. The Johansens had tried to be as generous as possible, but they cared for a number of children and weren't exactly rich. And I'd wanted to save money for the important things.

The driver gave me a wave, and I turned back toward campus. I scanned the buildings and swallowed hard. They were beautiful. Red brick with white accents. They looked important, stately, and I worried again about fitting in.

I adjusted the duffel on my shoulder before forcing my feet to move. It wasn't like not fitting in was anything I wasn't used to. I'd always been the odd one out. I'd had a few casual friends in high school, but no one I was truly close with. It was as if my classmates feared that someone losing their family was contagious.

Looking around, I searched for signs of the student center. I'd practically memorized the welcome packet from the number of times I'd gone over it. I'd looked at the map of campus more times than I could count, too, but it was different actually being here. Or maybe it was my horrible sense of direction.

I caught sight of what looked like a directory and headed toward it.

The paths through campus were brick, too, almost giving them a cobblestone feel. You could sense the history of the space all around you. I'd love to get lost in all that history and learn about it as I got used to my new home.

Stopping in front of the large map, I tried to orient myself. It took a second to find the *You Are Here* star and plot out a path to the student center, but the trek wouldn't be that far.

A bubble of excitement rose inside me, and I grinned as I turned to head for the center. But instead, I ran smack into what felt like a cinder block wall.

CHAPTER TWO

Hayden

I LET OUT A MUFFLED "OOMPH" AS I COLLIDED WITH THE foreign body.

"Shit," a rich voice muttered as large hands curved around my shoulders to keep me from falling.

That voice. It sounded like smoky promise and comfort all rolled into one. I had the bizarre urge to burrow into it. To roll around like I was a dog who'd found a deliciously muddy puddle.

"You okay? I didn't hurt you, did I?" the rich voice asked.

I blinked a few times, trying to clear my vision. It had gone just a bit hazy. As the guy in front of me came into focus, I just kept blinking. As if that would somehow make him less handsome.

My head craned way back to fully take him in. I wasn't tall by any stretch. A hint over five foot three on a good day. But this guy had to have a foot on me.

His sandy brown hair was laced with natural gold highlights that spoke of lots of time in the sunshine. His green eyes were kissed with flecks of gold in a pattern that had me wanting to lean in a little

He was hands down one of the most gorgeous men I'd ever seen. He screamed captain of the football team or fraternity president. Someone who would never be in my orbit.

"Sorry," I squeaked.

Worry creased his brow, his voice gentling as he released me. "Are you okay?"

I felt the strange sensation of loss as his warm hands disappeared from my shoulders.

My face heated. "Totally fine. Sorry. I wasn't watching where I was going."

"No worries," he said with a smile. "Freshman?"

I nodded. "I was just looking for the student center."

"Well, I'm headed that way. I can show you. Wouldn't want any more head-on collisions."

My blush deepened. "You don't have to."

He shrugged carelessly, which pulled the T-shirt he wore taut across his muscled chest. "I don't mind. I'm Knox, by the way."

The wind picked up, blowing my blonde hair into my face, and I hurried to brush it out of the way.

Knox's nostrils flared, and his green gaze went wide. "Where's your protection?"

I blinked up at him. "My protection?"

Was this guy some sort of creep who thought I was going to sleep with him because he showed me the way to the student center?

He glanced around quickly before lowering his voice. "Your guards."

A laugh burst out of me. "Do most students come with a secret service detail or something?"

This time it was Knox doing the blinking. His brow furrowed as he studied me, then he shifted uncomfortably before forcing a smile. "Figured it might take a full security detail to keep you concussion free."

My lips twitched. "Jerk."

He grinned, but there was still some unease in those gorgeous green eyes. "Come on. I'll play bodyguard from here to the student center."

"You really don't have to." But I fell into step beside him.

"I'm heading to the bookstore anyway. So, you're stuck with me."

Like that was a hardship.

As we made our way farther into campus, more students appeared. Their gazes all zeroed in on Knox. Guys offered him chin lifts and fist bumps, while girls gave him shy smiles or come-hither stares. Everyone seemed to know his name. Then their gazes would shift to me in puzzlement.

I didn't blame them. I didn't fit. Not in my favorite worn T-shirt that read, *If life gives you mold, make Penicillin,* and my scuffed-up Vans. I cringed. I really should've thought more about my arrival attire.

Knox glanced down at me. "You never said what your name was."

"Hayden. Hayden Parrish."

"Nice to meet you, Hayden Parrish. Where are you from?"

"A suburb of Seattle." The actual town name didn't matter.

"Welcome to Evergreen. It's pretty laid-back here. A good mix of people."

I nodded, toying with a loose thread on my T-shirt. "It's beautiful. How long have you gone here?"

"Since freshman year. I'm a junior now."

Made sense why he knew everyone.

"What dorm did you get?" Knox asked.

"Ridge Hall." I was used to sharing a room, but anxiety still bubbled at the unknown of who my roommate would be.

His gorgeous mouth curved. "That's a good one. It was renovated about five years ago."

I nodded, unsure of what else to say.

Knox wasn't put off. "What are you majoring in? Do you know?"

"Pre-med."

He let out a low whistle. "A brainiac."

Heat crept up my neck. "I just like science."

That wasn't completely true. I loved the subject, sure, but it was more. It was as though I thought if I learned medicine now, I could go back in time and save my mom and dad. I knew it was silly, but I needed to learn it. To understand how to heal the body. And if I couldn't save them, at least I could save others.

Knox's footsteps faltered. "What's wrong?"

"Huh?" I jolted out of my spiraling thoughts.

"You went somewhere. Didn't seem like an especially happy place."

So, Knox wasn't just a pretty face. He was astute and paid attention.

"I'm fine. Just taking it all in."

Annoyance passed across his face. He opened his mouth to ask another question, but I cut him off.

"I see the check-in tables. Thanks for showing me the way and saving me from first-day concussions. See you around, Knox."

I booked it for the check-in line before he could say another word. But more importantly, before he could ask another question. Because with those probing eyes and enticing voice, Knox could get me to divulge all my secrets.

CHAPTER THREE

Knox

I STARED AFTER THE GIRL AS SHE WOUND THROUGH THE crowd of students to find her appropriate line. *Hayden.* My mouth formed the moniker without giving it voice. I couldn't get myself to move my gaze away from that gorgeous blonde hair. But it was her violet eyes that were a sucker punch to the solar plexus. I'd never seen anything like them.

A protectiveness surged somewhere deep. A push to go after her, to stay close.

I took a deep breath. There were still hints of her in the air. She was fresh jasmine on a dewy morning. But there was more. She smelled like—

"Gallagher," a deep voice said as a hand clapped my shoulder. "What're you doing hanging around the frosh?"

I glanced over at my teammate. "Hey, Frank. Just heading to get my books."

But my gaze pulled back to Hayden. I didn't like her in that line alone. And I really didn't fucking like that the kid two spots behind her in line was checking out her ass. My back teeth ground together. I didn't blame him. Hayden's ass was stellar, but I still had the urge to rip his eyeballs from his head.

"Earth to Knox," Frank singsonged.

I jerked my gaze back to him. "Sorry, what?"

"Are you okay, dude? You having a stroke or something?"

A chuckle sounded to my right. "He's panting after a freshman already."

I turned annoyed eyes to my other teammate. "Fuck off, Jason."

But I couldn't help looking back at Hayden. She'd made it further up the line, but there were even more people around her now. It made me twitchy. She was so tiny, vulnerable. She needed someone watching her back.

Frank's gaze followed mine. "Damn. Not your usual type, but I see the appeal. Small, but she's got some curves on her."

A red film covered my vision, and I struggled to keep my breathing under control. *Shit.* I could not lose it. Not now. Not here.

I'd worked on control since I was a little boy. Tons of exercise to keep my beast just the slightest bit tired. Meditation to keep him calm. But none of that was helping right now.

I let my claws elongate just the slightest amount, pricking them into my palm. Pain was the best plan of attack to get me out of a rage state. Otherwise, I'd end up doing something regrettable, like gutting my friend in the middle of the quad.

"Uh, Frank. You might want to avert your gaze. Knox looks like he's about to remove your head from your body," Jason warned.

Frank jerked his focus back to me, his eyes widening. He held up both hands. "Shit, man. I meant no harm. Didn't know it was like that."

"Stay away from her," I gritted out. My voice held a growl that had Frank taking a step back.

Jason smacked me on the back. "Chill, dude. He's not making a move on your girl."

Your girl.

I liked that too much. Something about it just sounded *right*.

I tried to shake off the thought, cracking my neck. "She just doesn't need a walking hard-on making a pass at her."

Jason snorted. "Who does?"

"You're both assholes," Frank shot back.

Jason cast me a sidelong look. "Who is she, anyway?"

I shifted uncomfortably. I didn't want anyone looking too closely at Hayden. That could be a recipe for disaster, especially if what I suspected was true. "Not sure. Just met her today."

"Someone's a tad bit possessive for just meeting the chick today," Frank grumbled.

A hint of red was back in my vision, but I breathed through it, letting it pass. "She seems like a nice girl, that's all."

Frank and Jason went quiet for a moment, staring at me, dumbfounded.

It was Jason who finally spoke. "A *nice girl*? Are you a pod person? Tell me the truth. Is the real Knox up on some spaceship getting anally probed?"

I gave him a shove. "Piss off."

Frank snorted. "I don't know, a little ass play's nice sometimes."

"You two need to get a life."

Jason grinned. "Now, why would we do that when yours is clearly so much more interesting?"

They had no clue how right they were. Sure, we were friends. As much as I had human friends. We shot the shit. Mostly talking about football and classes and girls. But it never went past that surface level. It couldn't. Not when I had too much to hide.

We'd never have the kind of relationship I had with my brothers. Brothers forged in blood and battle. Brothers who knew me down to my soul. Brothers I needed to call about my possible discovery.

"Come on, let's get books before you're tempted to propose to the frosh you've known for two-point-five seconds," Frank chided.

I scowled at him. "I'm gonna shove a textbook up your ass if you don't watch it."

"Careful," Jason warned. "He said he likes ass play."

I just shook my head and started toward the student center and the bookstore inside. But my gaze pulled to the side yet again. Hayden was at one of the tables now, talking to a sophomore who was handing her a packet. I wanted to rip his arm out of the socket.

I needed to make that call and now.

I inclined my head toward the building. "I'll meet you inside. I gotta call Mad real quick."

"Tell the professor to take it easy on me this year," Frank muttered.

"I do that, and he'll grade you twice as hard."

Frank cursed. "Never mind. Should've known your friendship didn't have any perks."

I chuckled as he and Jason headed inside. Pulling out my phone, I hit Maddox's contact. He answered on the second ring. "Knox."

"We might have a problem."

Maddox was instantly on alert. "What kind of *problem*?"

My jaw worked back and forth, trying to think of how to explain. "I met a girl."

Maddox sighed. "I'm prepping lesson plans. Can we talk about your love life when we get home?"

I let out a low growl. "This is important."

He was quiet for a moment, then simply said, "Tell me."

"I—she—she crashed into me on campus. New freshman. I didn't realize it at first, but then the wind shifted. I scented her. Mad, she smelled like one of us."

CHAPTER FOUR

Hayden

I swore I felt eyes on me as I moved through campus. There was that telltale itch at the back of my neck. But when I turned around, no one was there.

Thankfully, the packet I'd been given with my temporary student ID, key card, and class schedule also had a map. I'd memorized the path between the student center and Ridge Hall before shoving it into my bag. I didn't need to advertise just how bad my sense of direction was.

I made my way down the brick path. There was some sort of frisbee game happening on one of the grassy areas, and a group of girls sat on a blanket, talking and laughing. I wondered if I'd ever have that. Friends. A sense of true belonging.

There was a chance here. A chance to start fresh. To erase the hard past and become someone new.

A sign on the building up ahead held my dorm's name. It was just as beautiful as all the other buildings. It held that same air of prestigious history.

Reaching into my back pocket, I pulled out my key card and

swiped it over the reader. The red light flashed to green, and I opened the door. There was a lounge to my right, where a couple of students were chatting and eating pizza. They all seemed perfectly at ease in their new surroundings. No first-day jitters like the ones thrumming through my body. Or maybe they were just better at faking it.

I headed for the staircase, rubbing a spot along my sternum. Knox had that same ease. As if he were completely comfortable with who he was. Of course, he was. Gorgeous and charming was the kind of combination that likely meant life came easy for him.

I gave my head a little shake. He was older and had an established group of friends, from what I glimpsed while waiting in line. I likely wouldn't see him again for months, even though the school was relatively small.

Reaching the third floor, I searched the doors for room numbers. Three-zero-three was what I needed. My packet told me that my roommate's name was Delaney Barlow. But that was all I knew about her.

I headed in the wrong direction at first and had to turn around. A few bends in the hallway later, I found an open door. Girls' excited chatter spilled out into the hallway.

Peeking at the number on the open door, I saw I was in the right place. A cascade of nerves tumbled through me. Forcing a smile, I stepped inside. The chatter came to a stop as three girls looked up at me.

A blonde was perched in a desk chair, leaning back on two of the legs. A redhead and a brunette sat on a bed that had perfectly matched bedding in a pretty, floral design. There were matching pillow shams and even a bucket chair in the corner made of the same material.

Everything about the image was perfect. Everything about it said I didn't fit.

The brunette leaned forward, her eyes roaming over me assessingly. "Hayden?"

I nodded. "Hi. Are you Delaney?"

"Yeah." Her lips pursed as soon as she spoke the single word. "I hope you don't mind. I just picked a side. I wanted to get set up."

"Sure. That's no problem." I preferred the side I'd gotten anyway. While hers had more space and a bigger closet, there was a window next to my bed. I'd be able to see out to the beautiful forests surrounding the campus.

"This is Maggie and Bella." Delaney inclined her head to the blonde and then the redhead.

"Nice to meet you," I greeted.

They looked at me with that same assessing stare as their friend. And they, too, didn't seem to like what they saw. They made polite noises of greeting, but the welcome didn't reach their eyes.

I bit the inside of my cheek and turned toward my bed.

"Are your parents bringing up the rest of your stuff?" Delaney asked.

It was a completely normal question; she'd have no way of knowing that it cut me to the core.

I didn't turn to face her when I answered. "I sent my stuff ahead."

I motioned to a large box that sat near the second desk in the room. All that was in it was bedding, but Delaney didn't need to know that.

"That's it?" Bella asked disbelievingly.

Maggie gaped at me. "What about all your shoes?"

My brows pulled together. "My shoes?"

"I had an entire box of just shoes. What are you going to wear to all the welcome parties?" Maggie seemed generally appalled on my behalf.

I shrugged. "I'm not really a partier."

Delaney scoffed, sifting her fingers through her silky, dark brown locks. "Your loss."

Maggie grinned. "More of the Irish boys for us."

My brow furrowed deeper, but I didn't bother asking. I didn't want to know.

I set to work unpacking my meager belongings and making my bed. It wasn't long before I completely faded into the background for the girls on the other side of the room. I was good at that. Fading so completely that sometimes I wondered if I'd disappeared altogether.

"God, I'd give anything for them. Knox with his panty-dropping smile, Easton with that broody stare, and Cáel with that feral grin." Bella practically moaned.

"Paws off Knox. I called dibs," Delaney snapped.

The weirdest sensation ripped through me at the sound of Knox's name on their lips. I wanted to claw her, scratch her eyes out, or do whatever it took to prove he was mine.

Maggie and Bella shared a look.

Delaney flicked her hair off her shoulder. "And I'd stay far away from Cáel. He'd be more likely to murder you than anything else."

"I'd like him to murder my vagina," Maggie muttered.

Delaney and Bella gaped at her.

She just shrugged. "What? He's got that whole Viking look going on, and I got really into that show over the summer."

They all dissolved into giggles.

Bella sent her friends a sly smile. "I heard they *share.*"

Delaney frowned. "A house? Sure. They live off campus."

"No. They share women," Bella whispered.

Heat flushed over my skin at the thought. Were the two other boys I'd seen with Knox earlier who they were talking about? Those boys had seemed so normal, average in comparison to Knox.

Delaney shook her head. "That has to be a lie."

Bella picked a piece of invisible lint off Delaney's comforter. "It's just what I heard. And Maddox and Cillian get in on it, too."

"There's no way," Maggie argued. "Maddox is a *professor* here. You know they have strict rules about that. He wouldn't risk it." Her mouth turned up at the corners. "Not that I wouldn't volunteer as tribute."

Laughter found them again, but I couldn't stop thinking about what Bella had suggested. Five men and one woman. What a hell of a lucky woman she would be.

CHAPTER FIVE

Hayden

I PRESSED DOWN HARDER ON THE WOUND, BUT THE BLOOD KEPT *pouring from my mother's chest. "Please, Mom. Don't leave me."*

I jolted upright in bed. My oversized T-shirt, damp with sweat, clung to my body. "Just a dream," I whispered to myself.

Only it wasn't. It was a memory that I was destined to relive over and over. There were times when I wouldn't have a nightmare for as long as a couple of months. But other times, they came every single night.

It was usually in seasons of change or when there were other stressors. I'd say that starting a new school hundreds of miles away from any home I'd ever known was a stressor.

I rubbed my eyes and swung my legs over the side of the bed, slipping my feet into flip-flops. Delaney snored softly in the bed next to mine. She had the blankets half over herself, but she'd obviously passed out in her clothes from last night—a black spandex miniskirt and sequined top.

She'd stumbled into the room after three in the morning, giggling and bumping into things. If this was going to be a regular occurrence, I was going to have to see about getting an apartment. But that meant I needed a job.

Pushing out of bed, I grabbed my shower caddy and headed for the bathrooms. Knox was right. This dorm was nice. The bathrooms were clearly newer, and the bedrooms had everything you'd need.

I made quick work of showering and brushing my teeth. I even took time to blow-dry my hair before heading back to my room. Delaney was still asleep when I stepped inside.

I tried to be as quiet as possible as I made my bed and went about finding an outfit to wear. I opted for a worn pair of jeans and another favorite T-shirt. This one spelled out *NErDy* in the periodic elements: nitrogen, erbium, and dysprosium.

A smile tugged at my lips as I pulled it on. I was who I was, and it was better for people to know that going in. I grabbed my now-empty backpack, shoved my wallet into the front pouch, and slipped my phone into my back pocket.

First stop of the day was the bookstore. Thankfully, books were covered under my scholarship, and I even had a small stipend for school supplies. But my scholarship was also contingent on keeping a 3.5 grade point average. That meant I needed to focus.

I pushed open the door and was hit with surprisingly cool air. I guessed that the higher elevation really did make a difference. I thought about heading back up to my room to grab a sweatshirt but didn't want to waste the time. Instead, I headed out into the sunshine and toward the student center.

"Hayden," a deep voice called.

I turned to see Knox striding toward me. He wore school warm-ups and a hoodie but somehow was able to make it look like the height of fashion.

"Hey," I said, my voice unsure.

He just grinned and extended a coffee holder. "I was coming to find you. I wasn't sure what you drank, so I brought options.

Black coffee. Coffee with cream and sugar. One of those caramel coffee drinks that are more like a milkshake. And hot chocolate."

I stared back at him, my jaw going just the slightest bit slack. "You brought me four different drinks?"

Knox nodded. "Seemed like the best move."

"Why?"

"I told you. I didn't know what you liked."

"No, why bring me anything at all?" My eyes narrowed on him. "Is this some weird hazing thing where there's ex-lax in my drink?"

Knox's lips twitched, and the gold in his eyes seemed to sparkle in the morning light. "I thought it would be a nice welcome. A gesture of friendship."

The word *friendship* had a pit settling in my stomach, but I forced a smile. "Then thank you, I guess."

I tugged the hot chocolate free from the container. "I hate coffee. Why on earth would anyone actually *want* to drink that bitter stuff?"

Knox dumped the other drinks into a nearby trash can and held up his own cup. "Because it's the nectar of the gods."

I shook my head. "That was a real waste of drinks and money."

He shrugged. "It was necessary." He pulled a paper bag out of his duffel. "Muffin?"

My brows pulled together as I took the offered treat. "This really is a full-stop shop over here."

Knox grinned back at me, and it was devastating. "We aim to please. Where are you heading so early? I thought I'd be able to catch you in your pj's." His brows waggled at that.

I snorted and began walking. "That's a little creepy."

"A man can dream, right?"

I just shook my head. "I'm going to the bookstore."

"Nice. I'll come with."

I shot him a sidelong look. "Why are you being so nice to me?"

Knox's steps faltered. "You seem like good people."

Such a simple answer, but somehow, not quite believable.

His eyes narrowed as his gaze swept over me. "Where's your coat or sweatshirt?"

I started walking again. "I didn't realize it would be this cold. It was warm yesterday."

Knox let out what almost sounded like a low growl and stormed over to a nearby table. Setting down his coffee and duffel, he pulled off his sweatshirt. I was talking one of those one-handed, grab-the-sweatshirt-from-behind-his-head kind of things.

It made his T-shirt ride up, exposing tanned abdominals and one of those V-things I thought were only in movies. I struggled not to swallow my tongue.

Knox shoved the sweatshirt in my direction. "Put this on."

"What? No. This is yours. Then you'll be cold."

"I just worked out. I'm fine."

With abs like that, of course, he had.

"Hayden…" Knox warned in a low voice that had a pleasant shiver cascading over me.

"Fine, fine." I set down my hot chocolate and muffin.

Knox handed me the sweatshirt, his fingertips brushing mine. The second they touched, a zap of electricity coursed through me. My vision tunneled. And then I was falling.

CHAPTER SIX

Hayden

K NOX CURSED AS HIS STRONG ARMS CAUGHT ME, LOWERING
me into a chair.

I blinked a few times as the world came back into focus. Knox knelt in front of me, his hands framing my face, a mixture of worry and wonder in his expression.

"Are you okay?" he asked, his voice rough.

I nodded slowly. "Sorry. I must have low blood sugar or something."

"Or something." I thought I heard Knox mutter under his breath.

His hands dropped away from my face, and then he pulled the sweatshirt over my head. "You need to get warm. And then you're going to eat every bite of that muffin and drink all the hot chocolate."

I arched an eyebrow at him as I pushed my arms through the sleeves of his sweatshirt. It was still warm from the heat of Knox's body. And the smell? It was like fresh pine after a hard rain. I wanted to live in that scent.

"Eat," he clipped.

"Enough with the orders, caveman," I snapped back.

Knox's expression gentled. "Sorry. I'm just worried about you." He nudged the muffin closer to me. "I thought you were going to pass out cold."

Seeing the genuine worry in his eyes, I broke off a piece of the muffin and popped it into my mouth. The lemon flavor burst on my tongue, and I couldn't help the little moan that escaped. "This is amazing."

I looked up to see Knox's eyes had gone completely gold.

He jerked his focus away from me and toward something in the distance. When he looked back, they were back to the same green with flecks of gold.

I blinked a few times. I was officially losing it.

Knox sat in the chair next to mine and flicked his gaze to the muffin pointedly.

"Okay, okay." I took another few bites, and the tension in Knox's shoulders began to ease.

"Where is your family from originally?" he asked once the muffin was half gone.

My stomach pitched. "I grew up in Maine when I was little, then the Seattle area."

What I didn't share was that it was a family friend of my parents who had brought me to Washington. I'd thought they were going to take me in but had placed me in foster care instead, saying it was *"for the best"*.

Knox tapped out a beat on the table as if puzzling that through. "What about your lineage?"

My brows furrowed as I ate another bite of the muffin. "Like ancestry?" What an odd question.

Knox nodded. "Yeah." He smiled, but it didn't read as authentic. "I'm Irish, through and through."

"I honestly don't know." When I'd been a kid, that kind of thing hadn't interested me. Now, I didn't have anyone to ask.

Knox's brows pulled together. "Your parents never talk about it?"

"My parents are dead. They were killed when I was eleven."

I said the words completely deadpan. As if the fact created no emotion in me at all. In reality, it fueled the kind of storm that would never end.

Knox's face went pale. This would be the end. People didn't like when things got real or when you reminded them of all they had to lose. In a few minutes, Knox would make some excuse—a practice he forgot about, a meeting, or breakfast with a friend. He'd leave, and I'd never see him again.

But that didn't happen. Instead, Knox did something that shocked me. He took his hand in mine, linking our fingers. The move was so smooth and natural it was as if he'd been doing it every day of both our lives.

"I'm so sorry, Hayden. I know what it's like to lose someone you love. I know it changes you. I hate that you've had to go through that."

I blinked a few times, staring into those beautiful green eyes. There was nothing but truth there. He did know. And that knowing made me feel truly seen for the first time in years.

"I'm sorry for you, too." My voice was barely a whisper, but Knox heard me. His fingers spasmed around mine.

"Who were you with after you lost your parents?" he asked.

I broke away from Knox's gaze, not wanting to see pity there. "My parents didn't have any living family—"

"Yo, Gallagher," one of the boys from yesterday called.

Knox's nostrils flared as annoyance filled his gaze. His fingers dropped mine as he spoke. "Hey."

The loss of his touch stung in more than one way. His comforting heat. The fact that he didn't want his friend to see him touching me. I fought the urge to curl in on myself.

The lanky boy sidled up to our table with a grin. "And what lovely lady do we have here?"

"Jason…" Knox said in a low warning.

That only made the guy smile wider, to the point that he looked slightly deranged. "I don't think we've met. I'm Jason. This one's much more charming and handsome friend."

I couldn't help the laugh that bubbled out of me. "Hayden. It's nice to know not all the guys around here are cavemen."

Jason barked out a laugh. "Making a real good impression, huh, Knox?"

"Shut up," he mumbled.

Jason's eyes danced as he held out a hand for me to shake. "Nice to meet you, Hayden."

Knox stood, batting Jason's hand away and letting out what sounded like a low growl. "Fuck off, J."

Jason just laughed, holding up both hands and backing away. "Touchy, touchy, touchy." Then he shot me a grin. "I'll be seeing you around, Hayden."

Knox let out another low, angry sound.

I stared at Knox as his chest rose and fell in ragged pants. "Did you just growl at him?"

Knox's gaze swung to me, and I swore it flashed gold again. "He was being annoying."

"You don't think that might be a wee bit extreme?" I asked, fighting a laugh.

"He's a punk," Knox grumbled as he sat again. Then he glared at my muffin. "You didn't finish eating."

I couldn't help it this time. I laughed. "I think you might need to take a nap. Or maybe you need this other half of the muffin. You might be hangry."

I broke off a piece and offered it to him.

Knox's gaze zeroed in on the muffin, but instead of taking it with his fingers, he bent down, closing his lips around my fingers and sucking the bite free.

Sparks of sensation zipped up my arm, and my eyes went wide as I sucked in a sharp breath.

Knox swallowed and grinned. "You're right. I feel a lot better."

I didn't. I felt like my skin was suddenly too tight for my body. I didn't know whether to run or throw myself at him.

A throat cleared. I jerked my gaze away from Knox and looked up and up until I reached a bizarrely familiar face. Even through the thick scruff, I could tell that the jaw had the same angular bend as Knox's. His nose and cheeks were identical, too. His hair was piled into a man bun on top of his head, but it was the same color as Knox's.

But the eyes were different. Green and gold, yes. But the gold flecks had a different pattern and shape. And the eyes themselves held so much disdain it dripped like acid.

"I'm guessing you're the piece of ass my brother won't shut up about."

CHAPTER SEVEN

Easton

THOSE VIOLET EYES FLARED IN SURPRISE AT MY WORDS, hurt even. Knox had described those eyes in infinite detail. He hadn't stopped droning on and on about the girl for the past twelve hours. But even with his incessant chatter, he hadn't done them justice.

They were a purple that seemed to change shades in the light, going deeper and then flaring brighter with emotion. Her blonde hair hung in waves around her shoulders. Hair that I could picture wrapping around my fist as I—

"What the hell, East?" Knox snarled.

I flicked my gaze in my twin's direction. I knew him better than anyone, and I could see his anger starting to build. The tension lining his shoulders, the way his breathing came just a bit quicker.

It wasn't a game I should be playing, pushing Knox's buttons. The only one with a quicker trigger than him was Cáel. And Cáel didn't have emotions besides rage and nothingness.

My lips twitched. "What? I can't say hello to your little *friend*?"

I said the word as if something smelled bad. And it did. The scent of the girl was too pure, too enticing. Jasmine, dew, and *us*.

Fuck.

Knox had been right about one thing, the girl had to be one of our kind. And from the confusion on her face right now, she had no bloody idea.

"You can if you aren't going to be an asshole," Knox snarled. "But that seems like an impossible feat these days."

He wasn't wrong. There was so much anger brewing inside me that it had started to spill out, lashing at the people I was closest to. And when they played with fire, like Knox was now, it was even worse.

I gave a casual shrug. "Just being honest. Got your panties in a twist over this one. Not your usual game."

The girl pushed to her feet, grabbing her backpack and the paper cup. "I'm going to let you two deal with whatever *this* is." She looked to Knox, her expression softening. "Thanks for breakfast."

I scoffed. "*Breakfast.*" My brother was a fucking idiot.

She turned those violet eyes to me. "I'd say it was nice to meet you, but I don't make a habit of lying."

I grinned at her, but it was all teeth. So, the kitten had claws after all. "See you around."

"God, I hope not," she mumbled as she headed down the stone path.

I was so caught up in watching her, the sway of her hips and the way her blonde hair caught the light as she walked, I didn't see the fist coming.

Knox didn't pull the punch. It connected with a force that meant I'd likely have to shift to heal it. The crack echoed in my ears as my entire body lurched to the side.

"Fuck, Knox," I snarled.

He moved to level another blow, but I side-stepped it, my eyes bleeding to gold. "I'll give you that one, but that's it."

"You're lucky I don't gut you where you stand," he growled.

My eyes flared. "You're going to let a piece of ass come between us?"

He charged, taking me down in a tackle that had us landing in the grass. We rolled and tussled, each landing various blows until shouts sounded.

"Jesus!" Frank muttered as he grabbed me by my shirt.

I could've thrown him across the quad if I'd wanted. But we'd learned time and time again to hide our gifts from humans. Even knowing that, it took everything I had to let him pull me back.

Jason had my brother by his T-shirt, creating more distance between us. "What the hell, you guys?"

I shoved out of Frank's hold. "None of your damn business."

I had no interest in these idiots. Knox liked to play the human role. Football team. *Friends.* I had no need for it. I'd rather have a small circle that truly knew me. My brothers.

But now, it seemed I could be losing that, too.

Knox struggled to get his breathing under control, and I knew by his clenched fists that his claws had elongated as he battled his fury.

Fuck.

What was wrong with me? Risking Knox's exposure wasn't something I'd ever want to do. But I had.

Knox jerked his chin at Jason. "I'm good. But I need to talk to my brother."

Frank and Jason eyed us warily. When neither of us lunged, Jason smacked Knox on the shoulder. "Don't let Coach catch you fighting. He'll bench you for sure."

"I know," Knox muttered.

I grimaced. Bench him? Who the hell cared?

Knox stayed still until Jason and Frank rounded the corner. Then he stalked toward me. "If you ever call Hayden a piece of ass again, I will do a hell of a lot more than punch you."

My back teeth ground together. "What the fuck's wrong with you?"

"What's wrong with me is that she's our *mate*," he snarled.

Everything in me locked. Blood roared in my ears as everything went cold. So damn cold it was a miracle I didn't fracture on the spot.

"You're wrong." My voice didn't sound like my own, foreign and far away.

Knox's jaw worked back and forth. "I know what a mating bond feels like, East. We've heard about it all our lives. I felt it. That zap of electricity. The extreme possessiveness."

Sweat gathered along my spine. "You just think you felt it. You want it so damn bad you're imagining it."

Knox's eyes flashed gold. "I'm not a moron. I know what I felt. And that means I'll do whatever it takes to protect her. Even if that means from *you*."

There it was. The line in the sand. Finding a mate changed everything. And not always for the better. Sometimes finding a mate meant having your whole world ripped out from under you.

CHAPTER EIGHT

Hayden

THE PLASTIC BAGS FULL TO THE BRIM WITH BOOKS CUT into my palms. But the hint of pain didn't distract me from the annoyance still bubbling down deep. Knox's twin was an asshole.

His instant hatred of me didn't make any sense. I'd never even met him before. Yet, he was acting as if I'd stolen his favorite teddy bear.

My lips curved at the thought of the massive guy cuddling a stuffed animal.

Something inside me shifted, a warmth filtering through. I shoved it down. There were no warm and fuzzies when it came to Mr. Grumpy Cat. It didn't matter that he was gorgeous, and I had a burning urge to pull the tie from that man bun. To know what it felt like to run my fingers through his hair.

My steps faltered, and I squeezed my eyes closed. "Nope. Nope. Nope."

I was not going to be a dumb girl. I'd made that move once in high school, believing the sweet lies of a boy who only wanted one thing. After he'd gotten it, I'd been dropped like the piece of trash he actually thought I was.

Not happening again.

I forced my eyes open and took a deep breath. My fingers had lost feeling somewhere between the student center and my dorm. *Shit.*

Picking up my pace, I moved in the direction of Ridge Hall. Getting all my books had taken hours. Even though I'd gotten to the bookstore early, there were already quite a few students with the same idea, and only two staff members were working. But I'd finally gotten everything I needed and secured a study desk in the library. Given my roommate's interest in partying, I had a feeling that I'd be spending quite a lot of time within the library's walls.

I didn't mind it. The library had always been a safe haven for me. And this one was stunning, just like the rest of the campus.

As I reached my dorm, a guy barreled out of the front door.

"Wait," I called. "Can you hold it?"

He paused, his eyes roaming over me. "Sure thing, beautiful. What's the password?"

I rolled my eyes. "The password is *I'll bean you with these books if you stare at my ass.*"

He barked out a laugh. "Might be worth it."

I just shook my head as I passed. College was definitely different. A sense of pride swept over me as I headed up the stairs. Hadn't today been *normal*? Aside from Grumpy Cat, that was.

I'd wanted normal for so long, and I was finally getting it. That felt amazing.

By the time I reached my room, I was huffing and puffing. I needed to take up jogging or make a visit to the gym on campus. This was getting pathetic.

Setting one bag down, I pulled my key card out of my back pocket and swiped it over the pad. The light flashed green, and I opened the door.

At the sound, Delaney whirled around from her spot at her

desk. Except it wasn't really a desk anymore. She'd transformed it into a vanity of sorts, with a massive lighted mirror and more makeup and hair products than I'd ever seen outside of a beauty store.

"Where have you been?" she clipped.

I blinked a few times as I crossed to my bed, setting down the bags and sliding off my backpack. "Uh, I went to get my books and to the library. Did we have plans I didn't know about?"

Delaney's jaw tightened, her mouth barely opening as she spoke. "I heard you had coffee with Knox Gallagher this morning."

Gallagher. I finally had his last name. It fit. His full name packed a punch, just like the man himself.

"Well?" Delaney pushed.

"Well, what?" I asked as I began organizing my textbooks on the tiny desk next to my bed. I wasn't sure they were all going to fit. I was taking a full load this semester, and each class seemed to be in competition for the thickest book.

Delaney let out a strangled noise. "Did you have coffee with Knox?"

I glanced at my raven-haired roomie. She'd obviously slept off her hangover. She looked perfect now. Dark hair curled, makeup expertly applied. She wore leggings and a sweater that clung to her curves in a way that wasn't showy but still hinted at what was beneath it.

I couldn't help but look down at myself. I wore ratty jeans, scuffed-up Vans, and Knox's sweatshirt that came to my knees. I wanted to wince.

"Um, yeah. I guess."

"You guess?" she shrieked. "The whole campus is talking about it. Do you know him from home or something? Why didn't you tell me? You need to invite him to do something with us."

I sucked in a breath and stumbled back a step. The girl's eyes were wild with desperation. "I don't really know him. He just helped me when I was lost yesterday, and then I ran into him this morning."

Leaving out the fact that he'd been heading to our room to find me seemed like a good idea at the current juncture.

Delaney's amber eyes narrowed on me, and her nostrils flared. "Is. That. His. Sweatshirt?"

I froze. Did I lie?

"It has his number on the back," she snapped.

Crap.

"I, uh, forgot my jacket. He was just being nice."

"Tell me everything from beginning to end. Right now," Delaney demanded.

I winced. The idea of sharing the few moments of true kindness I'd experienced from Knox today felt wrong. It was something I wanted to hold close to my chest.

"It really wasn't any big thing," I lied. Knox's kindness had been everything to me. "He showed me the way to the student center yesterday, and we talked about school today."

Delaney scoffed. "I hardly think Knox Gallagher is going to go on and on about *classes.*"

"Do you know him or something?" I asked.

A hint of pink hit her cheeks. "My sister's a junior. She knows them all. And when I visited last year, I met Knox. We really *connected.*"

The way she accentuated the word had nausea rolling through me. "Oh."

"Yeah, I'm just waiting to let him know I'm here. Wouldn't want to be desperate."

Delaney eyed me as she spoke, silently communicating that was exactly what she thought I was.

A knock sounded on the door, breaking her stare. I moved to answer it, grateful for the interruption. I opened the door to find a familiar face.

Knox grinned at me, and my belly hollowed out. He held up a plastic bag. "I brought lunch."

CHAPTER NINE

Hayden

THOSE GOLD FLECKS SEEMED TO GLINT UNDER THE fluorescent lights, twinkling all the more as Knox smiled wider. "You gonna let me in or what?"

I swallowed hard, taking a step back. "Sure…"

Knox came in, his gaze sweeping over the space. He gave Delaney a polite nod and kept right on going, studying my side of the room intently. "We gotta get you some posters or something. Make this homier."

Posters? That was what he was focused on?

"Knox," Delaney breathed in a husky voice. "It's *so* good to see you again." She looked up at him through fluttering lashes.

His mouth pulled down in a hint of a frown. "Have we met?"

I choked on a laugh, trying to turn it into a cough as Delaney's face went beet red.

"Of course. Bryce is my older sister. We met at the football party last year when I was visiting."

"Oh, yeah. Bryce is good people," Knox said.

I didn't miss that he hadn't remembered meeting Delaney. It was petty, but there was a tiny rush of relief at that.

Still, Delaney beamed at him as if Knox had told her he'd been counting down the days to her arrival. "She's the best. We should all get drinks at Ashes & Emeralds one night."

Knox shifted. "Maybe."

Delaney wasn't deterred. "We could go tonight."

Knox's gaze shifted to me for a second. "Uh, I've got plans tonight."

"Maybe this weekend, then?" Delaney pushed.

"Maybe," Knox echoed.

She stood from her chair, smiling widely. "Maybe you could show me around campus this afternoon. I'd love an insider's tour."

Knox moved back a step. "I'm sure Bryce would be great at that."

He turned to me before she could say another word. "Hayden, I was thinking we could eat outside. It warmed up a bit."

Anger burned through Delaney's gaze, landing directly on me.

"Uh, sure," I muttered, grabbing my wallet and key card.

Knox nodded at Delaney. "Good to see you again."

Her rage-filled expression instantly morphed into a simpering warmth. "You, too, Knox. I'm sure we'll be seeing a lot more of each other now."

A weird territorial feeling surged up inside me. I didn't want Delaney to see Knox. Which was the most ridiculous thought ever. I didn't get to control who Knox was friends with or who he was more than friends with, for that matter. We barely knew each other.

I ducked out into the hallway, and Knox shut the door behind us, letting out a hiss of breath. Our eyes locked, and we both laughed.

I tried to muffle it as I hurried down the hall. "Are you trying to get me murdered in my sleep?" I hissed at him.

"She's, uh...intense."

I sighed. "I think you're high on her list of priorities this semester."

Knox groaned as we stepped into the stairwell. "Why are girls so weird sometimes?"

My lips twitched. "It's a real hardship to be loved and adored, huh?"

Something passed over Knox's expression. "She doesn't even know me."

My steps faltered as I really took him in. I had no doubt that Knox had girls all over campus interested in him. From the pieces I'd put together, he was a football player on top of his good looks, which only added to the appeal. But if that was all people saw in you, the attention would feel pretty damn empty.

"I'm sorry," I whispered.

Knox's gaze snapped to mine. "For what?"

"Laughing about Delaney. It has to get old, that kind of attention. Maybe even feel lonely."

Knox moved a bit closer, so near that I could feel the heat wafting off his body. "Lonely's the exact right word."

"I'm sorry."

Knox's gaze dropped to my lips. "Hayden—"

A door slammed above us, jolting us out of the moment.

Knox muttered something under his breath. He pressed a hand to the small of my back. "Come on, before your roomie hunts us down."

I bit back a chuckle and let him guide me down the stairs. I still wore his sweatshirt, but I could feel the heat from his hand practically scalding my skin. I'd never been more aware of someone, every minute shift of his body.

When we got outside, I moved just out of touching distance. Contact with Knox was too damn dangerous.

"There are some tables over by the academic buildings that should be quiet right now," Knox said softly, his gaze still locked on me.

"Sure. I've got a meeting with my advisor in a bit, so that's perfect."

We were quiet as we walked. The few students we passed all greeted Knox by name. And I noticed that he was kind to everyone. It didn't matter what the person looked like or where they might fall in the social hierarchy, he smiled and answered with a hello or a question. I liked that about him. The judgment-free zone.

We reached a smaller quad where only a couple of other students were present, and Knox inclined his head toward an empty table. "This good?"

I nodded. "You didn't have to bring me lunch. You already brought me breakfast."

He scowled. "Breakfast that got rudely interrupted. This is an apology for Easton."

Easton. The name fit him somehow. Equal parts prestigious and wild.

"You don't have to apologize for someone else's actions," I said as I sat.

"Yes, I do. He's got a complicated history. I swear he's not as awful as he seems at first. It just takes him time to trust people."

I frowned at that. It sounded like there was a story there. But the reasons behind something didn't matter; the actions were what counted. "I've been calling him Mr. Grumpy Cat in my head."

Knox barked out a laugh. "That's kind of perfect."

I grinned. "He has the same scowl as that damn meme."

Knox shook his head as he pulled out two wrapped sandwiches, handing me one. "Scarily accurate. What about you? Any siblings?"

"No. It's just me." Which meant I'd been all that more alone after my parents died.

Knox shifted in his seat, seeming to choose his words carefully. "What happened to your parents?"

It was a bold and nosy question. Especially for someone who didn't really know me, but I appreciated it somehow. That Knox simply asked what he wanted to know instead of probing around the subject.

It wasn't something I talked about. Not ever. But somehow, I didn't mind giving Knox the truth, even though just thinking the words made my stomach hurt.

"They were murdered."

CHAPTER TEN

Hayden

K NOX'S ENTIRE BODY STIFFENED, AND I SWORE HIS EYES flashed gold. "Murdered?"

I nodded, dropping my gaze from his. I couldn't handle seeing other people's reactions. Not when their emotions only amplified my own. "When I was eleven."

"Hayden." Knox's voice was strangled, garbled. "I'm so sorry."

I picked at a loose thread on my jeans. "Me, too."

His large hand covered mine, and a buzz lit beneath my skin. "Who took care of you after?"

I bit my bottom lip, wishing I could avoid this part of the conversation. "I didn't have anyone. I thought maybe this friend of my parents would take me in, but they couldn't handle a kid. I ended up in the system."

Knox's hand clenched around mine. "Foster care?"

I nodded. "It wasn't that bad. I got lucky with my third placement. The Johansens were really kind. They even let me stay after my eighteenth birthday so that I could finish high school."

The only sound was that of Knox's ragged breathing, as if he were struggling for control.

It forced my gaze away from my lap and toward those beautiful green eyes. There was only one word to describe the emotion there. Anguish.

"You were alone," he gritted out.

I shrugged. "Aren't lots of people?"

"You shouldn't have been alone."

How many times had I wished I'd had someone? Anyone who *really* knew me. "Maybe, but I got through it."

Knox's eyes searched mine as if looking for any hint of a lie. "You're not going to be alone anymore."

I stilled. What did that mean? It seemed like a hell of a promise from someone who didn't know me at all. Unease trickled through me, and I pulled my hand free. I'd known someone else who'd made similar promises, and he'd bolted the second he'd taken my virginity.

Hurt flashed across Knox's expression, but it was quickly replaced by determination. "I just know what it's like to lose the people you love. But I had East. He might be a cantankerous fucker, but he's my twin, and I know he'll always have my back."

I studied Knox for a moment, looking for any hints of deception, but I didn't sense anything. "Who did you lose?"

A hardness settled into his jaw.

"You don't have to tell me—"

"No. I want to. I just—I don't talk about it much. My whole family. Parents. Little sister. Older brother. They all died in a, uh, fire." Knox's gaze shifted away as if he, too, couldn't take my reaction to his revelation.

God, I couldn't imagine losing that many people in a single moment. "I'm so sorry."

He swallowed, his Adam's apple bobbing with the action. "It's why East can be a prick sometimes. He doesn't like to let himself care about anyone any more than he has to."

A niggle of guilt worked its way into my belly. I didn't want to feel empathy for the jerk from this morning, but I found my heart aching for not only Knox but for Easton, too. "I hate that you guys went through that."

Knox turned back, his eyes locking with mine. "It changes you, doesn't it? Grief?"

I nodded. I'd lost track of all the impacts losing my parents had on me. Everything from my pre-med quest to never feeling like I fit in. It made me a different person than I was before. But it also meant I never missed an opportunity to be grateful for the little things. A beautiful sunrise, a boy bringing me lunch and sharing his truth. Because I knew how easily it could all be ripped away.

"It does change you. For the better and the worse all at the same time."

His eyes held mine, not letting go. "I guess that's true. Sometimes, I think I only see the bad."

I traced a pattern on my jeans. "Even the worst things on the planet can still result in good. It doesn't make the price worth it, but I think it helps to see those gifts, nonetheless."

Knox leaned back in his chair, letting out a whoosh of breath. "You're pretty amazing. You know that?"

My gaze flicked to his in question.

"You've been through so much, but you're still here, looking for the bright spots."

I shrugged. "I don't want to look for the shadows. I already know they're there."

Knox's expression went stormy at my words. "No more shadows."

I couldn't help it. I laughed. "Life is full of them."

"Not for you. Not anymore."

I grinned at him. "I love that you think you can just erase them."

"Not just think. I can. I've got your back, Hayden."

There was such determination in Knox's voice, such certainty.

I shook my head, sending him a puzzled look. "Why do you care?"

He was quiet for a moment. "I don't know. I guess I just got an instant good vibe from you. I think we were meant to be friends. Don't you?"

Friends.

I hated the disappointment that flared to life in my chest at the word. But I also understood the pull Knox was talking about. There was this tug toward the guy next to me. He felt like safety and comfort…home. It was such a bizarre thought, but I couldn't ignore that it was present.

"Maybe we were meant to be friends."

An affronted look swept across Knox's face. "*Maybe?*"

I chuckled. "Okay, our best friendship was written in the stars."

"That's a little better."

"Knox," a deep voice called.

Sensation swept across my skin at the tenor. The tone was almost musical. I was turning before I'd given my body the command to do so, as if my entire form just had to see who the voice belonged to.

Looking up, my jaw went slack. The man who walked toward our table looked more like he should've been gracing the cover of *GQ* than walking the pathways of this tiny university. He was tall with broad shoulders and a leanly muscled frame, like that of an Olympic swimmer. His hair was jet black. Just a bit long, styled in an artfully messy way. His olive skin made the amber of his eyes glow warmer, and dark stubble dotted his jawline. As he approached, his nostrils flared, his gaze locking on me.

Knox cleared his throat. "Mad, this is Hayden. Hayden, this is one of my brothers, Maddox."

The man stopped in front of me, and I extended a hand on instinct. "Nice to meet you."

My voice sounded robotic and just a bit high-pitched.

"You, too." Maddox's brows furrowed as his large hand engulfed mine.

The second our palms touched, it was as if lightning shot through me. That same phantom wave as when Knox had touched me the first time. My vision tunneled, and darkness tried to swallow me whole.

CHAPTER ELEVEN

Maddox

THE GIRL'S EYES FLARED AS THE VIOLET IN HER GAZE flashed molten.

Holy hell.

The mate bond sang through my nerve endings, leaving behind third-degree burns I'd take over and over again. The inferno sparked a mixture of lust and protectiveness and knowing.

How many times had I heard the true-mate bond described? More than I could count. From my own parents and from the elders in our horde. But all their stories paled in comparison to what I felt now.

I wanted to scoop up Hayden in my arms and carry her back to our den. All I could see were a million potential dangers around us. Things I *had* to protect her from.

Hayden's eyes fluttered, and she began to list sideways. I quickly dropped her hand and moved to steady her.

Knox rushed to her other side. "Shit. Hayden, are you okay?"

She blinked rapidly, coming back to herself. "Sorry. I don't know—that's the second time that's happened today. Maybe I should go to the health center."

I dropped my hand from her shoulder as though the contact scalded me. *Health center*. Hayden was a student.

I gritted my teeth. My mate was over a decade younger than me and so beyond off-limits, it wasn't even funny. The university had strict rules about fraternizing with students. I'd always thought it was a good rule. Until now.

"I think you just need to eat a little something. You probably have low blood sugar," Knox couched, moving a sandwich closer to her.

"Yeah, maybe." Hayden unwrapped the meal, her long, delicate fingers moving in graceful motions.

She glanced up at me, a gorgeous blush staining her pale cheeks. "Sorry about that. Not the greatest first impression."

God, I wanted to touch her. To hold her in my arms and assure her that there wasn't a damn thing she could do that would make me love her any less.

"No problem." My voice was deeper than normal, raspier. "But you should make sure you're getting enough to eat."

A million questions swam through my brain. Did she have enough to eat? Was she warm enough? Was she happy?

Amusement lightened those violet eyes. "You guys have a real thing about food."

Knox grunted.

Understatement of the century. When our kind found their mate, they had a deeply ingrained need to make sure their mate was safe and cared for. To provide for them in every way imaginable. Food was just the tip of the iceberg.

Hayden took a small bite of her sandwich. Watching her mouth move was a recipe for disaster. I had to force my gaze back to her eyes. "You're a freshman this year?"

She nodded, swallowing and taking a sip of the soda Knox handed her. "Yes. And you're…"

Her words trailed off as if confused.

My lips twitched. "I'm a professor here."

Hayden's brow furrowed as she glanced at Knox. "You called him your brother."

Knox grinned. "Not by blood. More by choice. There are five of us that live together. Old family friends. You'll meet them all."

I could barely swallow my groan. Our bond was going to eat this girl alive. She was tiny and delicate, with clearly no idea of what we were or what she was. How was that possible?

"Oh," Hayden murmured. "It's nice that you have that."

There was an undisguised longing in her voice, a yearning to belong. An ache lit deep in my chest. My mate had felt alone, that much was clear.

"You'll have it now, too," Knox assured her.

Hayden's eyes flared in surprise, and I sent him a look of warning. She wouldn't understand why Knox was so quickly trying to bring her into the fold. If he moved too fast, he could scare Hayden off, and that was the last thing we needed.

She picked at her sandwich. "It'd be nice to meet your friends."

I wanted to laugh. She said it as if we were some sort of childhood playgroup. But she had no idea.

Knox grinned. "They're going to love you."

Hayden glanced down at her watch. "Crap! I have to be at the meeting with my advisor in five minutes."

Knox scowled as she quickly rose. "You didn't eat your sandwich."

"I'll eat it after." Hayden quickly wrapped it up and took off toward the science building. "Thanks for lunch. Nice to meet you, Maddox."

My gut tightened at the sound of my name on her lips. Perfect berry pink lips—shit. I had to shut that down. But I still watched her until she disappeared inside.

Knox shoved me. "I told you."

My gaze jerked to him. "She doesn't show any sign of scenting us."

Knox's expression darkened. "Her parents were killed, murdered. She ended up in foster care."

Rage sparked to life from somewhere deep, a blazing inferno almost impossible to tamp down.

"Mad, your eyes," Knox warned.

I closed them, working to get myself under control. I breathed deep, going to that Zen place I always did when my beast tried to take the reins. But he wanted to rage for his mate, to defend her and annihilate anyone who had caused her pain.

When I finally opened my eyes again, I was back in control.

"This is going to be tricky," Knox muttered. "How the hell are we going to explain it to her?"

I didn't have the first clue. "We have to tread carefully. And I can't be involved."

Knox gaped at me. "She's our mate."

"And she's a student at this university. I can't touch her for at least four years."

Knox's jaw only dropped further. "Mad, you'll be in agony."

He was right. Staying away from your mate went against every instinct we had. It could cause physical pain, even sickness. "I don't have a choice."

He shook his head. "That's dumb—"

"Don't," I clipped. "Let's focus on the more important things. We need to make sure she's safe. Protected." I sighed. "We need to call Cillian."

Our alpha had been back East, dealing with family drama, but he needed to know this.

Knox sent me a worried look. "We have to tell Cáel. He's going to lose it."

I winced. Cáel wasn't altogether stable. He'd been too broken for that. And I wasn't sure what a mate bond would do to him. He might gut every man that looked at Hayden. What a hell of a mess that would be to clean up.

CHAPTER TWELVE

Hayden

"Oops," Delaney muttered as my pile of books tumbled to the floor.

Her lips twitched as she headed to the door, not bothering to pick up what she'd so clearly meant to knock over.

I sighed as I crouched to pick up the books and papers. Delaney had made it clear over the past twenty-four hours that I was on her shit list. That was fine, but this petty, mean-girl crap was already getting old.

Shoving everything into my backpack, I zipped it closed. Or I would've if the zipper hadn't caught halfway on its path. I worked it with my fingers, but it wouldn't budge. The cheap pull snapped free, and I let loose a few creative curses.

I really hoped this wasn't an omen for my first day of classes. I tugged the zipper with my fingers, even though the pull was missing. It worked okay. But I knew I needed a backpack. It was also a reminder that I needed a job ASAP.

Sighing, I pushed to my feet and slung my backpack over my shoulder. My hand hovered over the sweatshirt folded on my desk

There'd been a big part of me that had wanted to put on Knox's hoodie as a source of comfort and armor. But I wasn't sure what he would've thought if he saw me in it.

I shook the thought free and headed for the door. When I'd gotten to my advisor's office yesterday, there'd been a note rescheduling our meeting for this morning. While it was slightly annoying, I didn't mind that I'd been pulled away from Knox and Maddox.

Everything about them was…*intense*. As if being too close in proximity to both of them at the same time made my body go haywire.

I shook my head as I opened the door and stepped out into the sunshine. I guessed I wasn't used to being around such gorgeous guys. There must have been something in the water in Ember Hollow.

I hurried through campus, thankful I at least knew my way, thanks to Knox's field trip yesterday. While campus was now crowded, most people didn't pay me any mind. I did catch a few girls glancing my way or whispering to their friends as I passed. The actions made my stomach cramp. I really hoped Delaney hadn't spread some ugly rumor out of spite.

Picking up my pace, I headed up the steps to the science building. The outside had the same brick façade as the others, but the interior was much newer and brighter. I couldn't wait to see what the labs looked like.

I slipped in behind another student and made my way to the hallways that housed the 300 offices.

Checking each one as I passed, I finally came to a stop before an open door. I peeked inside and saw a middle-aged man typing away on a computer.

I lifted my hand and knocked on the door.

"Come in," the man said without looking up.

I walked toward an open chair opposite his desk. "Professor Brent?"

His typing slowed, and he finally looked up. He was probably in his mid-fifties, with brown hair and a bit of salt and pepper woven through it. His hazel eyes swept over me.

Something about the way he assessed me sent a shiver down my spine. "Hayden Parrish?"

I nodded. "Yes, sir."

Those hazel eyes flashed. "Sit."

I did as he instructed, sliding my backpack from my shoulders and placing it next to my chair.

Professor Brent pulled a file from his stack, scanning the first page quickly. "Quite the scholarship you snagged."

I didn't say anything. It wasn't exactly a question, so I wasn't sure what he was looking for.

His gaze lifted. "You're going to have to keep your average above a 3.5, and you're taking a heavy load this semester."

"I know. My classes are my number one priority. So, I don't think it will be an issue."

Brent traced a hand over his lower lip as he studied me, and I fought the urge to squirm. "I like to do more frequent check-ins with my scholarship advisees. I want to make sure we catch any slip-ups before it's too late."

I swallowed hard. The idea of losing my scholarship was just about the worst thing I could imagine. "Okay."

"We'll start with every other week for now. Adjust from there."

That seemed like a lot of check-ins. But if it would keep me on track, that was all right with me. "Sure."

Brent's gaze was intense on my face. "You've already declared pre-med. You're sure about that major? It's one of the most challenging at the university."

"I'm sure. I've wanted to be a doctor since I was eleven."

He pushed his chair back and stood, rounded his desk so that he was standing next to me, and leaned back against the mahogany. His leg grazed mine as he shifted, but he made no move to break the contact.

I coughed, using the action to lean away and create distance.

Brent's eyes narrowed. "With such big goals, you're lucky you landed me as an advisor. I've coached many students through their MCAT exams and into prestigious medical schools."

A wave of nausea swept through me as he moved slightly closer again.

"Thank you, Professor." I made a show of checking my watch. "I don't want to be late for bio. I better be going."

Annoyance flitted over his features. "You have Kavanaugh?"

I nodded.

"I should have you transferred into my section for that," he muttered. "But I'll have you for Intro to Psychology, so that's something."

The way the professor spoke made my skin crawl, and I hurried to push to my feet, grabbing my backpack.

"Email me to set up our next meeting, Hayden."

"Of course, Professor." I didn't look at him as I bolted for the door.

I wondered if you could switch advisors. But changing would likely piss him off, and since he was going to be teaching another one of my classes, that didn't seem like the best idea.

I bit the inside of my lip as I hurried down the hall. I rounded the corner and ran smack into a hard wall of muscle. And then I was falling.

CHAPTER THIRTEEN

Hayden

A MUTTERED CURSE ECHOED IN THE EMPTY HALLWAY AS strong hands caught my flailing arms, keeping me from hitting the floor hard.

I blinked a few times, my heart hammering against my ribs as my vision came into focus. I was met with the image of a beautiful face twisted in disgust.

"Don't you watch where the hell you're going?" Easton snapped.

My hands trembled at my sides, the adrenaline from my meeting with Brent still humming through my system. I'd been mostly lucky when it came to foster placements, but that hadn't meant it was completely creeper free. I had a finely honed radar for sleazes for a reason. And being in such close proximity to Brent had sent the memories surging.

"Sorry," I muttered, trying to duck around Easton.

His hand flashed out quicker than should've been possible, and he caught my arm. "What happened?"

"Nothing," I muttered.

Easton's gaze dropped to my hands as if to call *bullshit*.

I quickly grasped them together in an attempt to hide the shaking. "It's not like you care. You'd probably be happier if a Mack truck mowed me down."

His green eyes narrowed, the gold flecks in them appearing to spark and shift. He took a step forward, his voice dropping lower. "What. *Happened*?"

After the scene in Brent's office, Easton's aggression should've had me shaking like a leaf. But I weirdly wasn't at all scared. I met his stare dead on. "I'll tell you what happened if you tell me why you hated me on sight."

Something passed over Easton's eyes so fast I couldn't pin down the emotion. "You're right. My life would be a hell of a lot easier if you got taken out by a Mack truck."

He turned on his heel and stalked down the hallway.

I stood there for a moment, just breathing, trying to slow my heart rate. What the hell was the matter with him? Mr. Grumpy Cat was exactly the right name for him.

More students appeared in the hallway, and I knew I needed to move. With one last deep breath, I went in search of my classroom. It only took me two wrong turns before I found it, but thankfully, I made it before the bell rang.

I'd always loved biology. It had been the science that had come most naturally to me. It was chemistry that was always a struggle. I hoped that this would be one of my easier classes, but as soon as I stepped inside the room, I knew that wouldn't be the case.

Angry green eyes locked with mine, and I nearly tripped over my own feet. Easton. But he was a junior. Shouldn't he have been in an upper-level science? I guessed not if he wasn't a science major.

He sat at a lab table next to another guy who was typing away on a cell phone. Across the aisle from him, my roommate chattered away. I didn't think he heard a word Delaney said. And when she realized she'd lost his attention, her gaze followed his line of focus. The moment Delaney caught sight of me, red rose in her cheeks, and a scowl twisted her pretty mouth.

Great. Just great. My favorite class was going to be ruined by two people who wanted to kill me with their eyes.

I hurried down the aisle, ducking my head and avoiding their stares. I slipped into an open chair at the back of the room. Looking over, there was a girl whose dark brown hair hung in her face.

She jolted as I sat.

"Is it okay if I sit here?" I asked.

She nodded in a staccato rhythm but didn't say a word.

At least she wasn't glaring at me.

"I'm Hayden," I said quietly.

"Wren," the girl said. Her voice had a husky quality to it, as if she didn't use it often.

"Nice to meet you."

She bobbed her head in a nod, and her hair shifted with the motion. It revealed a scar slashed across her cheek. I fought the urge to suck in a breath. Whatever had happened to her had to have hurt.

A voice cleared at the front of the room, jerking my focus in that direction.

"Good morning," a gravelly voice greeted.

That tenor. It skated over me in a pleasant shiver yet again as Maddox's gaze swept over the classroom.

"I'm Professor Kavanaugh, and this is Biology 101."

Oh, crap. Knox's hot-as-hell *brother* was my biology professor.

"Some of you are in this class because you're already planning a science major. Others are just trying to get a core education requirement fulfilled. Either way, I'll do my best to get you through this as painlessly as possible."

Students laughed, and I swore I heard a few girls sigh.

I scanned the room and didn't miss a few girls fluttering their lashes his way. A surge of anger swept through me, and I had to grip the desk to get myself under control.

Maddox's gaze snapped to me, as if he could somehow read my emotions. His jaw tensed, and he forced his focus to the stack of papers in front of him.

What the hell was wrong with me? It was as if every one of my emotions was in overdrive lately.

I tried again to focus on my breathing as Maddox discussed the class's syllabus, but it was a struggle. The words on my paper swirled and danced.

By the time class was over, I thought I'd only heard about half of what Maddox had said. I'd at least caught the reading we were supposed to do for homework. I needed to get it together by the time our class met next, or I was going to lose my scholarship for sure.

The bell rang, and I stuffed my notebook and the syllabus into my backpack. I didn't miss how Wren hovered at the back of the classroom until most of the students were gone and then made a beeline for the door. I frowned after her as I made my way up the aisle.

"Ms. Parrish," Maddox said, voice low.

My gaze jerked in his direction. "Yes?" The single word came out as more of a squeak.

"Are you all right? You seemed…distracted."

Crap. Crap. Triple crap.

"Sorry. I guess I'm still getting used to college life. I'll do better next class."

Maddox's eyes narrowed on me in a similar fashion as Easton's earlier. As if he were searching for any hints of a lie. "If you need help with anything, Knox would be happy to assist you."

Why did it sting that he wasn't offering his own assistance?

"I'm okay. Really. I'm excited about this class. I'll be more focused next time." I had to be.

A hint of amusement flickered in Maddox's amber eyes. "Be sure that you are, Ms. Parrish."

There was something about him using my last name. As if he were trying to create distance between us, but at the same time, the moniker held a sultry promise.

And I was pretty sure that an entire semester with Maddox as my professor might actually make me combust.

CHAPTER FOURTEEN

Hayden

MY EYES BURNED AS THE WIND WHIPPED AROUND ME, cutting through my flimsy jacket. I pulled it tighter around me as I headed off campus and toward Ember Hollow's picturesque downtown. The Old West feel would've been a lot more adorable if I wasn't exhausted.

My first day had been beyond long. I shared three classes with my roommate, who'd made a show of whispering loudly about me to her friends. Thankfully, I only had the one with Easton. But who knew what tomorrow would bring.

The workload at Evergreen was no joke. I'd have to stay up until midnight, at least, just to finish the reading. I didn't want to think about what would happen when tests and exams rolled around.

I turned onto Bitter Brush Street, the main thoroughfare through town. The wind stung my cheeks, and I picked up my pace. The sign for *Spark's Diner* had an adorable scrawl to it with little fireworks around the words.

I'd combed the classifieds over lunch, and this was the best opening available. I just hoped my four years of waitressing experience would land me the gig.

Grabbing the handle, I opened the door, an antique bell tinkling. I quickly stepped inside and let the warmth swirl around me. There were a few groups of students at booths and a mother with two young kids, but the space was far from crowded.

"How can I help ya, darlin'?" a husky female voice asked.

My gaze moved to the owner of the voice. She looked to be in her sixties or seventies, with lines around her eyes, and white combed through her blonde hair that was pulled back in a braid.

I crossed to the counter, forcing a wide smile. "I'd like to apply for the waitress position."

As I got closer, the woman's nostrils flared, and her eyes widened. "Al-all right." She cleared her throat. "I'm Fiona, and this is my place."

"Nice to meet you, Fiona. I'm Hayden. I worked in a café for four years back home." I slid my backpack off my shoulder and worked open my falling-apart zipper to pull out a piece of paper. "Here's my résumé with references."

Fiona's brows lifted as she took the paper. "Very professional."

I shrugged. "I need a job. I wanted to give myself the best shot."

Something in the woman's expression softened at that, and she turned to scan the sheet. "Looks good to me. When can you start?"

I blinked a few times. "That's it?"

She shrugged. "You know how to work a register?"

I nodded.

"Can you carry a tray without dropping it?"

I nodded again.

"That's all I need. When can you start?"

"Now, if you want." Relief coursed through me. One less thing to have on my worry list.

"Perfect. Come on back, and I'll show you the lockers."

I followed Fiona down a narrow hallway until she paused at a closed door.

"There's a code to get into the staff room. Three-three-two-eight. Memorize it or put it into your phone."

I pulled out my cell and plugged it into the Notes app, just in case.

Fiona led me inside and opened one of the six lockers. "You can use this. There's an apron inside. Don't need to wear anything fancy for work, but no T-shirts with profanity or miniskirts where I can see your underwear."

I choked on a laugh. "Is that usually a problem?"

She rolled her eyes. "Some of these kids today. Makes me feel old."

I understood the sentiment. Sometimes, being faced with Delaney made me feel decades older than my fellow students.

"Get that apron on, and I'll show you the ropes," Fiona said.

I quickly slipped my backpack inside the locker and donned the turquoise apron with *Spark's* written in cursive letters across the front.

"Ready," I said, turning to face her.

"You're quick, I'll give you that."

I met Fiona's stare. "I'll work hard. I promise."

"We'll see," she muttered.

I thought I'd won her over with my résumé and need for a job, but maybe I still had work to do.

Fiona showed me around the diner, listing off table numbers and how the floor was split into sections. "It's gonna pick up real soon. That three o'clock hour is full of students, and it'll stay busy until we close at nine. On weekends, we stay open until midnight. Get a nice business from students trying to eat away their drunkenness. You up for working weekends?"

"Yes, ma'am," I said quickly. I'd take all the hours I could get, and then I'd be spending the rest of the time in the library.

"Glad to hear it. Won't need you every weekend, but I'll work you in here and there. Rotating schedule."

I nodded. "I can make it work whenever you need me."

"Fair enough. There's your first table." Fiona nodded at a table of unfamiliar students.

I got to work, losing myself in the familiar rhythm of taking orders and delivering food. Fiona was right about the busyness factor. More and more students piled in through the doors. Most of the tables filled quickly, other than a single reserved table in my section.

I wiped down another table that had just been vacated, trying to make room for a group waiting to be seated, when movement caught my eye through the window. A black Mercedes G-Wagon pulled into a spot right in front of the diner.

Nothing about the vehicle was run-of-the-mill. The windows were so dark you didn't have a prayer of seeing inside. The tires were slightly larger than normal, and the spokes were completely black, as well.

I half expected Secret Service agents to pile out of it. I was wrong.

The driver got out first. Easton still had his hair piled into that light brown man bun with gold woven through it. His face was set in a scowl as he slammed his door.

At least I knew his scowls weren't for me alone.

The passenger door opened, and Knox jumped out. He didn't have his usual grin in place, but he wasn't pissed off like his brother, either. He just looked stoically gorgeous.

I forced my gaze away, giving the table one last swipe and motioning to the group waiting by the door. As they sat, I took drink orders and handed out menus.

By the time I returned with their beverages, those two familiar faces were sitting at my reserved table. I approached warily. "Are you allowed to be sitting here?"

Knox's gaze jerked up at the sound of my voice, and a huge grin spread across his face. "Hayden, what are you doing here?"

Easton scoffed and simply glared in my direction.

Oh, joy.

I pointed at my apron. "I'll give you three guesses, but the first two don't count."

Knox frowned. "Aren't you taking a full course load? Are you sure you have time for a job?"

I pulled my menu pad out of my apron pocket. "I've managed work and school for a long time."

Apparently, that was the wrong thing to say, because Knox's frown only deepened.

"You shouldn't be working here," Easton gritted out.

My gaze flicked to him. "And why's that?"

His jaw worked back and forth. "It's not the place for you. Try on campus. The bookstore or something. Or just stick to your classes."

My eyes narrowed. "Not everyone gets to roll around in G-Wagons for fun. Some of us have to provide for ourselves."

Easton's green eyes flashed gold as he gnashed his teeth together.

Knox choked on a laugh. "Told you the Mercedes was too much." His focus moved to me, expression sobering. "Just don't push it too hard, okay? Don't want you getting sick or anything."

"I won't," I assured him. "Now, would you like something to drink?"

"Yeah. I'll have a—shit," Knox muttered. His gaze moved from somewhere on the street back to me. "I'm really sorry for what's about to happen."

CHAPTER FIFTEEN

Hayden

MY BROW FURROWED AT KNOX'S WORDS, BUT THE sound of the bell had me turning toward the door. As I took in the man in the entryway, I froze. I'd never seen anything like him. He looked like he was born in a different time. The Viking era, maybe?

He was massive, even taller than the twins, with broad shoulders and a muscled chest. His white-blond hair was long but shaved on the sides. The strands themselves were woven into intricate braids or dreads, and tattoos decorated the sides of his skull.

The moment his light blue eyes locked on me, they flashed silver.

He moved quickly then, his scuffed-up motorcycle boots eating up the space as he strode toward me.

My lips parted in part shock, part awe.

"Cáel," Knox warned.

But it was too late. The Viking came right into my space and hauled me into his arms, crushing me to his chest.

I let out an oomph at the impact. My first instinct was to shove him off or knee him in the balls. But the second his scent wrapped around me, I froze. It was a mix of freshly falling snow and campfire. Something about it held me captive, but more than that, it hit me with a longing that nearly took me out at the knees.

The man's hand slipped under my fall of hair, and the moment his fingers touched my neck, that now-familiar zap of electricity coursed through me. He shuddered against me, seeming to feel the exact same sensation I was.

"Ceann Beag," he whispered.

"Cáel," Easton growled. "Let her go."

"No," he gritted out.

Knox approached, and Cáel pulled me tighter against himself. "She doesn't know you, Cáel. You don't want to scare her."

He let out a shuddered breath, slowly releasing me.

When I was back on my feet, my legs wobbled.

Cáel's light blue eyes narrowed on me. "Did I scare you?"

"Uh, no?" It came out like a question instead of a statement.

"Good," he grunted.

Knox sighed, pinching the bridge of his nose. "Sit down, Cáel. I'll get our order in."

Cáel glared at Knox but slid into the booth. Easton didn't sit until he was completely settled.

"Come on," Knox whispered, guiding me with a hand on my lower back.

That was when I felt it. The eyes on me.

I quickly glanced around and saw that everyone in the diner was staring at me. "What did I do?" I whispered back.

Knox pushed me into the back hallway, away from prying eyes. "Are you okay?"

I tried to peek around his large form and back into the restaurant, but he moved to block my view.

"Hayden."

I looked up into those green eyes so filled with concern. "I'm fine. But that was…What was that?"

That concern morphed into pain. "Cáel. He's one of our brothers. But he doesn't always act like most people. A lot of kids on campus are scared of him."

Pain lanced my chest. "I know what it's like to not feel normal," I said quietly.

With all the eyes that had been on me a few moments ago, I could only imagine how Cáel felt all the time.

Knox wrapped his arms around me, pulling me into his chest. "I'm so sorry, Hayden."

"I'm fine," I mumbled. "I just meant that I get it."

Knox kept hold of me but pulled back a fraction so that he could meet my eyes. "I told him about you. How amazing you are. But I didn't expect *that*."

My brows pulled together in confusion.

"Cáel doesn't usually touch...anyone," Knox explained. "He can't handle the contact."

I sucked in a sharp breath. What would that be like? Not to be able to withstand any human contact.

I didn't get a lot of it. Even now, just having Knox's arms wrapped around me was an overload to my senses. But I'd had something. Mrs. Johansen would hug me on big occasions like my birthday or graduation. Mr. Johansen would pat me on the shoulder when I got an A on a test. Cáel had none of that.

My stomach twisted as I wondered what had happened to result in that need for complete touch deprivation. My eyes searched Knox's. "What happened to him?"

Knox's entire expression became a blank mask. "It's a long story."

I understood his not telling me. It wasn't any of my business. But that didn't change the fact that there was a part of me desperate to know.

Knox let out a long breath, but he didn't release me. "I'm not sure how he'll be going forward, but I have a feeling he's going to be pretty protective. Once he decides he likes someone, he doesn't deal well with any perceived threats against them."

My mouth curved. "Good thing I'm not on the run from the mafia, then."

One corner of Knox's mouth kicked up. "Good thing."

We stared at each other for another long moment.

"I won't hurt him," I whispered. "I promise."

A mixture of pain and relief swirled in Knox's eyes. "You're kind of a miracle, Hayden Parrish."

He leaned forward and pressed his lips to my forehead.

Sensation ripped through me at this simple touch. A cascade of sparks, as if a firework had been set off next to us.

I pulled back, and Knox's eyes swirled gold.

What the hell was that?

CHAPTER SIXTEEN

Hayden

I TRIED TO SHAKE OFF THE FEELING OF KNOX'S LIPS ON MY forehead, the flash of gold eyes in my mind. But the sensations of his touch still coursed through me. A faint buzz radiated through my muscles.

I did my best to ignore it as I placed another order for a new group of students that had come in.

"How are you doing so far?" Fiona asked as she added a second order next to mine on the wheel.

I forced a smile. "Good. You were right about the three o'clock hour. It's packed."

She nodded absently. "Busy's better. Makes the shifts go faster."

I knew she was right about that. The hours that dragged on were when there was hardly anyone to serve.

"How do you know Knox, Easton, and Cáel?" Fiona asked, her voice barely a whisper.

My brows pulled together. "Um, school?"

I said it like a question but hurried to explain. "I met Knox and Easton at school. I just, uh, met Cáel."

Fiona's eyes went wide, and her skin paled several shades. "You'd never met him before?"

I shook my head. "I guess Knox just told him about me."

Fiona gripped my arm and squeezed. "Just be careful. They're mixed up in things a girl like you doesn't want any part of."

I frowned as she grabbed two plates of food and headed for a table. What the hell did that mean?

I stole a quick glance at the table of guys. Cáel was staring in my direction. Knox elbowed him hard in the side, and he grunted.

"Order up," Ian, the cook, called as he shoved three massive plates of food across the pass-through window. "It's for the boys." He inclined his head toward the table I'd been looking at.

I bit my lip as I loaded my tray, trying to put the pieces together. My stomach flipped as I thought about Easton's fancy car. Maybe they were dealing drugs or something.

Balancing the heavy tray on my palm, I made my way toward their table. I carefully lowered it to call out their orders without making eye contact. "Two cheeseburgers, fries, and onion rings?"

"Me," Easton grunted.

I slid the plate in front of him.

"Steak, mashed potatoes, and a side of lasagna?"

"Here," Cáel growled.

The grit in his voice made me jump, my gaze snapping to his. The light blue hue of his eyes held me captive for a moment, my breaths coming faster. It was then I saw a faint scar bisecting his lip.

Cáel extended his hands toward me slowly. Tattoos extended from beneath his sleeves and covered his hands. But his movements were gentle, as if he didn't want to scare me.

I handed the plate to him, and his mouth curved the slightest amount.

"And the last one's mine," Knox said with a smile, but it seemed a little forced around the edges.

I slid the cheeseburger and BLT combo in front of him. "Hungry?"

Knox's grin widened, becoming more genuine. "We always are." He glanced around the space. "How's your first day going?"

I followed his gaze, noting a table that needed their orders taken. "Good. Fiona's really nice." And so far, the tables had left me pretty good tips.

"Good," Knox said. "What time do you get off?"

"I'm actually not sure."

He pulled out his phone. "What's your number?"

My brow furrowed.

Knox's fingers tapped the screen. "You shouldn't walk back to the dorm alone if it's dark. I can give you a ride."

"You don't have to—"

A low growl had my gaze snapping to Cáel.

"It's not safe," he gritted out.

"Okay," I acquiesced quickly and listed off my phone number.

Knox's fingers flew across the screen. "I just sent you a text so you have my number. Just call when you're getting close to being done."

"If it's dark," I muttered. "Do you guys need anything else to drink?"

They shook their heads, and I moved away, tucking my tray under my arm. I crossed to the table that needed to be served and forced a smile. "Welcome to Spark's. Can I get you guys anything to drink? Or are you ready to order?"

The table was full of guys wearing various Evergreen gear. They were all on the larger size but not nearly as big as my new friends.

One of them ran his gaze over me and grinned. "You on the menu?"

Gross.

"I'm afraid that's going to be a no, but the cheeseburger is pretty damn good."

His friends laughed, but he kept his eyes locked on me as they all ordered.

Great. I did not need to deal with creepy customers.

Placing their orders with Ian, I moved through my tables, cleaning empty ones or checking with patrons to see if they needed anything. It didn't take long before Ian was calling *order up* again.

I hurried back to the pass-through window and grabbed the plates, loading up my tray. I crossed back to the table of what I assumed were jocks and began unloading orders. Working at the café for the past four years had really helped with my memory, and I easily remembered who had ordered what.

A few of the guys were polite and thanked me, but some merely grunted. As I set the final plate in front of the creeper, a hand cupped my ass.

I jerked, stepping back and out of his grasp, glaring at him.

The guy just laughed. "Come on. Can't put it out there and not expect me to cop a feel."

One second, he was in the booth, and the next, he was being hauled into the air by his throat.

"Did. You. Touch. Her?" Cáel snarled, baring his teeth.

The guy's face went a ghostly shade of pale. "No. I mean, yeah. I mean, I didn't know you knew her."

Cáel's hand tightened around the guy's throat.

Knox cursed as he hurried over.

Easton followed but looked a hell of a lot more casual in his approach. "You don't touch *any* woman without their consent, limp dick."

The guy's face grew red, but his friends didn't make a move.

Knox moved toward Cáel. "Okay, you made your point. Let him go."

"No," Cáel gritted out.

"He can't breathe," Knox pushed. "We can't have a body on our hands."

Cáel's fingers tightened a fraction. "Hayden's under *my* protection. If any of you even look her way, I'll pull your spleen through your nose."

He released the guy, sending him stumbling back to the booth, then his gaze jerked to mine. Cáel's breathing was ragged as he started toward me, but Knox gave him a hard shove.

"No," Knox ordered. "Get in the SUV."

Cáel's eyes flashed silver, and Knox cursed.

Knox pushed Cáel toward the door, Easton following behind, dropping a few bills on the table. Easton's gaze met the table in front of me. "Remember what Cáel said. We might not be around to stop him next time."

Chapter Seventeen

Cáel

"**G**et in the fucking car," Knox snarled. My breaths came in ragged pants, and I was two seconds away from shifting. I couldn't leave her. Not now. Not in that diner with *them*.

The locks beeped, and Knox yanked open the back door of the G-Wagon. "I swear to God, Cáel. I will lock you in the basement if you don't get your shit together."

Easton scoffed. "A lot of good that'll do."

"We can't leave her." The words were more beast than human, and the twins cursed, shoving me into the back seat.

Knox got in after me, and Easton hauled ass to the driver's seat.

"We need distance. Now," Knox clipped.

"No shit, Sherlock," Easton snapped as the G-Wagon purred to life.

My chest expanded and contracted in painful bursts. Scales rippled across my arms.

"Faster!" Knox yelled, then he turned back to me. "Breathe, Cáel. You gotta breathe, or you're going to shift."

I tried to obey, to get my body under control, but all I could think about was the woman in the diner. She was so tiny. Delicate. Vulnerable. So easily hurt.

"Can't. Leave. Her," I wheezed, trying to hold my beast back.

"Go to the forest," Knox ordered Easton.

"I am," he clipped back.

Knox was careful not to touch me, but he got in my face. "I've got Ian looking out for her until I go back to pick her up. She's safe. Totally fine."

Easton made a sharp turn, dropping us onto a gravel road.

"He touched her," I gritted out.

Knox's eyes went gold, and I knew it sent him into just as much of a rage as it had me—someone's hand on *our* mate. He just had better control than I did.

"And he's been dealt with," Knox assured me. "He'll likely piss his pants the next time she walks across his path."

That should've been a relief, but it wasn't. I wanted to hunt. To *kill*.

I needed to end the threat to my mate. To make him *suffer* for thinking he could ever touch her.

Easton screeched to a halt, sending gravel flying. "Get him the hell out of my car before he torches it."

Knox opened the door, sliding out and giving me space to do the same.

I stumbled out of the vehicle, falling to my hands and knees. The shift was pleasure and pain in equal measure, but when you fought it happening, it was only pain. But I knew if I let my beast free right now, he'd go straight for the diner.

He'd rip the asshole to shreds and then take Hayden and never let her go.

"Jesus," Easton muttered.

"He's getting it under control," Knox shot back.

Easton began to pace, gripping the back of his neck. "This is exactly what I warned you about. The mate bond is already making him unstable. That's going to happen every time someone touches her."

Agony ripped through me. It wasn't just fighting the shift now; it was knowing that I was hurting my brother by not keeping it together. But the pain helped. It gave me a fraction more control.

Knox gritted his teeth. "It's going to be a period of adjustment. We'll all be more possessive than normal at first. More protective. But we'll find our rhythm again."

My breathing eased a fraction as I sat back on my heels.

Easton shook his head. "It'll be a disaster. It's going to end us."

Pain flashed in Knox's eyes. "We're not Ryan. What happened to him isn't going to happen to us."

Easton's gaze went gold. "Look at Cáel already. That's just when someone grabbed Hayden's ass. What happens if someone really hurts her? What if the worst happens?"

A red haze passed over my vision as fury pulsed through me. I felt the scales ripple over my skin, but I quickly called them back. Hayden was fine. She was safe. And we'd keep her that way.

As if Knox read my mind, he glared at Easton. "We're going to keep her safe. Nothing's going to happen to Hayden."

Easton just scoffed. "You might like to think you control the universe, but you don't. Anything could happen to her. When the supernatural community finds out what she is…"

Easton's words trailed off, but I knew what he was going to say. When people found out the truth, they'd want Hayden for themselves, to use her in any number of ways.

"That's why we're going to protect her," Knox snapped.

"How?" Easton challenged.

I pushed to my feet. "We bring her back to the compound. We can keep her safe there."

He turned to me. "And what are you going to tell her to get her there?"

I snapped my mouth closed. I didn't have the first clue.

"That's what I thought," Easton shot back.

"We keep going as we have been," Knox argued. "We be her *friend*. She's going to need us."

That was the understatement of the century. If it was true that Hayden had no clue what she was, then her whole world was about to be ripped apart.

Easton's jaw tightened. "She could be latent. This could all be for nothing."

It wouldn't matter if Hayden never shifted. She'd still be the most important being on the planet to me. But I didn't think that would be a problem. "I sensed power in her. Immense strength."

Knox's head jerked in my direction. "You did?"

I nodded. "She's an incredibly powerful dragon. She just doesn't know it."

CHAPTER EIGHTEEN

Hayden

ROCKS AND STICKS SLICED INTO MY BARE FEET AS I RAN. I pumped my arms and legs harder. Trying to get away. Trying to get safe.

"Càit a bheil a' bhana-phrionnsa?"

The voice bellowed into the night around me. Fear stabbed at me. I knew he was getting closer. Close enough that he could end me just like he ended my mother.

A roar sounded from the sky, and my gaze flew upward.

A massive silvery-white dragon sailed through the sky. I should've been terrified, but I wasn't.

The beast swooped down over me, landing in the path.

The man skidded to a halt. "Drágon adhair," he spat.

The giant creature opened his mouth, and a silver fire flew out, engulfing the man in flames. He screamed and writhed, but the dragon made no move to help him. Instead, he turned to me.

My heart hammered against my ribs, but I didn't move.

The white dragon moved closer and closer. As he did, I saw that his body was riddled with scars. Each one sliced at my heart. I wanted to lay my hands on each one. To heal them.

The dragon lowered his huge head so that it was level with me.

I reached my hand up, pressing it to his cheek. And I swore the dragon purred.

The beep of my alarm jerked me out of the dream, and I rolled over, fumbling for the off button. What a bizarre dream.

"Shut it off," Delaney grumbled.

I did, as quickly as possible, but stuck my tongue out at her, even if she couldn't see me.

When I'd gotten home from work last night, she'd pounced. I guessed word had already made the rounds about the scene with Cáel. Delaney had accused me of lying, saying I had to know the guys from somewhere else because there was no reason they'd be so protective of me otherwise.

In some ways, I understood. Their protectiveness didn't make sense. But I couldn't give her answers because I didn't have any. She hadn't been pleased.

Sliding out of bed, I made quick work of my morning routine and pulled out clothes. Today's T-shirt read, *Think like a proton. Stay positive.* I giggled to myself.

I would take all the little happies today because I felt like I'd run a marathon last night. Between yesterday's shift at Spark's and what felt like constant dreaming while I slept, I was exhausted.

I rubbed my fingers together. I swore I could still feel the warm scales beneath my fingertips.

Shaking myself out of the memory, I grabbed a sweater and wrapped it around myself, then my jacket. I shoved my notebooks and the textbooks I needed into my backpack and headed out the door.

I hurried down the steps and into the crisp fall air. But I came up short as a hulking figure stood from his perch at one of the tables outside my dorm.

Cáel really had the Viking look going for himself today. His white-blond hair caught the early morning sunlight, and his leather jacket gave him an extra air of badass he really didn't need. The tattoos curling up his neck and across the sides of his head did that for him.

He extended a cup to me. "Knox said you like hot chocolate."

My mouth curved as I took the cup. "I do. Thank you."

"I got you one of those chocolate croissants, too." His brow furrowed. "Do you like those? I could get you something else if you don't. I—"

"I love them. Anything chocolate, really." My heart squeezed at the massive man's struggle. He was trying so hard.

A smile spread across Cáel's face. It was a little rough around the edges, as if he didn't make the motion often. "I like chocolate, too."

I fell into step next to him. "Then I guess we have that in common."

He nodded, shoving his hands into his pockets.

"Are you heading to class?" I asked.

Cáel shook his head. "Library."

"Nice. Are you a junior like Knox and Easton?" I realized I hardly knew anything about the giant walking next to me.

"Senior."

I bit the inside of my cheek to keep from laughing. Conversation clearly didn't come naturally to him. "What are you majoring in?"

Cáel's light blue gaze flicked to me. "Engineering."

"Oh. Wow. That has to be intense."

He shrugged. "I like it. Black-and-white answers."

No shades of gray. I so got that. And for someone like Cáel, having a yes or no answer was probably comforting. "That can make things a lot easier."

Cáel bobbed his head in agreement but didn't say anything. Every so often, he would peek over at me as we walked. The third time, he scowled. "You need a warmer coat."

I glanced down at myself. The jacket I'd had for the past three years had been warm enough for Seattle, but I had to admit it wasn't quite doing the job in this higher elevation. "I'm going to get one after I get my first paycheck." There had to be a thrift shop around here somewhere that I could find a good deal.

Cáel's scowl only deepened. "You should get one now. You don't want to get sick."

I chuckled at his grumpiness. "You're giving Mr. Grumpy Cat a run for his money."

His spine snapped straight. "Huh?"

"Easton. He's always scowling and hissing. So, I call him Mr. Grumpy Cat in my head."

Cáel's lips twitched. "He know that?"

"Not unless Knox told him."

"I really want to be around when he finds out."

I choked on a laugh. "If he doesn't want insulting nicknames, he shouldn't be a jerk."

"Fair," Cáel muttered.

A group of guys approached us on the sidewalk, and one dipped his head in greeting.

Cáel let out a low growl, and the guy's eyes widened as he stumbled out of our path.

I turned to my giant friend. "What was that about?"

"They were too close," he gritted out.

I reached up, resting a hand on his arm. "He was just being friendly. I'm perfectly fine. I promise. And I know how to protect myself if someone wasn't friendly."

Cáel's nostrils flared, his breathing growing more ragged.

Crap. Maybe that had been the wrong thing to say.

He moved then, pulling me into his arms and holding me tight, almost sending my hot chocolate flying. "Nothing can happen to you, Little One."

Those words curled around me, comforting somehow.

I hugged Cáel back, sensing he needed it. "Nothing's going to happen to me."

"No," he growled. "It's not. Because I won't let it."

CHAPTER NINETEEN

Hayden

I TOOK A SEAT IN THE MIDDLE OF THE SMALL LECTURE HALL. There were more than a few familiar faces dotting the space. But none of them had gotten to even what I'd call acquaintance status. It seemed like a lot of students were keeping their distance from me. But that didn't stop their staring.

Opening my notebook, I jotted down the date and *Psychology 101*. I'd just focus on taking the world's best notes.

A chair squeaked on the opposite side of the aisle, and my gaze flicked in that direction. Green eyes met mine. They were guarded, but there was also anger there. Anger I didn't understand.

As much as I'd hoped Easton's warning to the guys in the diner had meant a softening toward me, that clearly wasn't the case. It was also obvious that he'd left any and all science requirements for the end of his school years if he was stuck in my classes.

His eyes narrowed on me. So, I did the only thing a mature person would do. I flipped him off.

Someone down my row choked on a laugh, which only made Easton glare harder.

Whatever. Mr. Grumpy Cat could scowl until his face froze like that, for all I cared.

"Everyone, find your seats," Professor Brent said as he crossed to the podium. His eyes scanned the room and paused on me, something flashing in his hazel gaze.

"This is Psychology 101. While it's a beginner class, I am going to expect a lot from you. If you were hoping for an easy A, I suggest heading to the registrar and transferring to another class. There are other professors who would take it easier on you."

There were a few grumbles from the seats around me, and I heard a muttered curse, but no one made a move to leave.

"All right, then, let's get started."

Professor Brent moved quickly through the syllabus and expectations. There was going to be a lot of reading, quite a few papers, and a couple of massive group projects. This would be one of my toughest classes, for sure. Not something I'd expected when planning for my semester.

Throughout the class, Professor Brent's eyes would land on me. Each time, they made me shiver, and not in a pleasant way. By the time the bell rang, my stomach was in knots. After this semester, I'd simply switch advisors and make sure I didn't take another class with Brent. I just had to make it through this term.

Closing my notebook, I shoved my belongings into my backpack and struggled to close the broken zipper. I slipped it over my shoulder and headed down the steps.

"Hayden, a moment please," Professor Brent said.

That twisting sensation was back in my stomach. "Yes, Professor?"

He watched as students filed out behind me. "I thought you were taking your studies seriously?"

I frowned. "I am."

"Then, why were you sitting in practically the back row? I'd think a serious student would be sitting in the front row."

My mouth went dry. Everything in me was screaming that I

needed distance from this man. "I see better from the middle of the classroom. It's more comfortable on my neck."

Brent's mouth pursed. "I see."

I didn't say anything, but his disapproval was clear.

"Make sure you don't get distracted by students who are messing around. I'd hate to see your focus slip."

Why did that feel like a threat?

"Hayden, you ready?" a deep voice called from behind me.

I glanced over my shoulder to see Easton standing there, a hard gaze locked on Professor Brent.

I glanced back at the professor. "Did you need anything else?"

Brent glared at Easton and then turned back to me. "Be sure to email me to set up our next meeting."

"Of course." But I was dreading it. I tried to think of any reason to miss the meeting or to bring someone with me, but nothing came to mind.

I started for the door, and Easton fell into step beside me.

"What the hell is that douche's deal?" he snarled.

"I don't know," I mumbled. "I think he just wants to make sure my focus is in the right place since I'm pre-med."

Easton's eyes flared. "You want to be a doctor?"

I nodded. "Since I was eleven."

He opened his mouth to say something and then shut it. His back teeth ground together. "Just keep your distance from Brent."

With that, Easton stormed off without another word.

Yeah, it would be super easy to stay away from my academic advisor, who wanted to meet twice a month in person, and whom I saw in class twice a week. I fought a groan.

"Hayden," a voice called from behind me, and I turned to see Knox jogging through the crowd of students.

When he reached me, he pulled me into a hug, inhaling deeply. "Missed you."

I laughed. "I saw you yesterday." But even saying that, it was as if my whole body relaxed in his hold, that pine and rain scent wrapping around me.

"Too long," he grumbled, finally releasing me. "Where are you headed?"

"Back to my dorm. I have a shift at Spark's."

Knox frowned. "What time are you off?"

"Five. Fiona has the dinner rush covered."

A grin spread across his face. "Perfect. I'll pick you up at the dorm at six."

It was my turn to frown. "For what?"

"You're coming to dinner at my house. All my brothers will be there, even Cillian."

My palms dampened. "I don't know…that sounds like family time." Because even if these guys weren't all blood related, it was clear they had created their own family.

Knox shook his head. "You're coming. Cill is dying to meet you, and I want to show you our place. *Please?*"

I couldn't resist the pleading tone of Knox's voice. "Okay. I just can't stay too late. This course load is going to kill me."

Worry flashed across Knox's expression. "Do you need help with any of your classes?"

I shook my head. "I just need time to study."

His mouth thinned. "Okay. I can study with you this weekend if you want. We can hole up in the library and only break for food."

Something shifted inside me. I couldn't remember if I'd ever had a friend who would offer to do that with me. Only, friendship wasn't exactly what I felt for Knox. For any of them. I shoved that thought down. "Sure. That'd be great."

He beamed at me. "Awesome. I'll see you at six."

"See you."

I walked back to my dorm in a bit of a haze. Knox and Cáel had made me feel unbelievably welcomed and accepted. It was everything I'd hoped for when I'd thought of starting college. Yet there was this part of me that wanted so much more.

I flashed my key card over the lock to my dorm room and stepped inside. I pulled up short as I took in my bed.

There were five different jackets laid out on the mattress. One looked like it would've prepared me for an excursion to the Arctic. Another was slightly thinner but still made of that puffy down material. The third was a bit more fashion-forward. It was army green but lined with some sort of insulation I knew would make it super warm. The fourth was a rain jacket that looked like it would protect me from torrential downpours. The fifth had an invisible fist squeezing my heart.

It was a gorgeous black leather motorcycle jacket. My fingers skimmed over the fabric. It was the softest thing I'd ever felt. I couldn't imagine how expensive it must've been. And its presence meant one thing.

Cáel.

CHAPTER TWENTY

Hayden

I THUMBED THROUGH MY CLOSET, SEARCHING FOR SOMETHING appropriate. But I didn't have the first clue what that might be. Grabbing my phone from the desk, I typed out a text, the first one I'd sent Knox.

Me: *What should I be wearing to this dinner?*

I tapped my fingers along the back of the device as three little dots appeared.

Knox: *Would it be wrong to say as little as possible?*

I choked on a laugh as my cheeks flamed.

Me: *Not helpful.*

Knox: *All right, then you should wear whatever you're comfortable in. There's no dress code. I'll see you in five.*

Crap. Five minutes wasn't enough time.

I dropped my phone back to the desk, pulled on a pair of jeans, and grabbed a sweater from my closet. It was a deep teal that made the violet in my eyes pop. I pulled it over my head and grabbed an older pair of boots in my closet. They'd been a secondhand shop find. The leather was worn, but it looked purposeful as opposed to falling apart.

"Where are you going?"

I stiffened at the accusation in Delaney's voice. "To dinner."

Her eyes narrowed in my direction. "With who?"

Triple crap.

I swallowed hard as I slipped on my boots. "Some friends."

Knox counted as a friend. Cáel, too. Therefore, I wasn't lying.

Delaney pushed off her bed. "You're going with Knox, aren't you?"

The accusation was back, as if I'd stolen her favorite sweater or something.

"Yes." I snatched my key card and wallet out of my backpack and moved back to the closet.

"Take me with you."

My stomach roiled as I reached for one of my new jackets, the army green one. "I think it's a family thing."

Delaney's jaw clenched. "You aren't family."

"No, but Knox wanted me to meet his family. I can't just bring someone along."

Her mouth formed a perfect little O. "He's taking you to his *house*?" she shrieked.

I pulled on my jacket and shoved my wallet and phone into the pocket. "Um, yeah."

"No one gets invited there. I haven't heard of a single classmate. Not once. My sister hasn't either."

My brow furrowed at that. Knox hadn't made it seem like a big deal, but maybe it was.

I shrugged. "I don't know."

Delaney grabbed my arm, squeezing it hard. "*Please*, Hayden. Just text him and ask if I can come."

My stomach gave another twist. "It would be rude. If you want to go to dinner with Knox, ask him."

Just the idea of it made me want to puke, but Knox was free to do whatever he wanted. He didn't owe me anything.

Delaney released her grip on me, glaring. "You're not going to make a whole lot of friends if you won't do someone a simple favor."

Her words landed, slicing into me, but I didn't reply. I moved for the door and headed out into the hallway. Each step had guilt digging deeper. By the time I reached the quad, I felt awful.

"Hayden," Knox called, pushing off a BMW X5.

I blinked a few times, pulling myself out of my spiraling thoughts. "Hi."

He frowned, wrapping his arms around me. "What's wrong?"

I shook my head. "Nothing."

Knox pinned me with a stare. "Hayden…"

I let out a whoosh of breath. "Delaney wants to come to dinner. She realized I was going with you and asked me to bring her. She kept pushing and really wanted to come. Now I feel like a jerk because I said no."

He studied me carefully, running a hand up and down my back. "Do you want her to come?"

I bit the inside of my cheek. "Not particularly."

Knox grinned. "Good. Because I gotta be honest, your roommate creeps me out a little."

I pressed my lips together to keep from laughing. "She has a crush on you."

Knox's face scrunched up. "She doesn't even know me."

And that had to burn. All these people wanted a piece of Knox but didn't have the first clue as to who he really was.

"Well, you are pretty to look at," I mumbled.

Knox's smile was back, wider this time. "Is that so?"

Heat hit my cheeks. "You know you are," I grumbled. "Too pretty for your own good."

Knox ducked his head and pressed a kiss to my temple. "Good to know."

My entire body lit at the brush of his lips against my skin.

"Come on. Don't want to keep my brothers waiting. They get hangry."

Flustered, I let Knox guide me toward his SUV and help me inside. In a matter of seconds, we were headed away from campus and into the forest.

"You live outside of town?" I asked.

Knox nodded. "We like having space. It's quieter. Peaceful."

I understood that. It was one of the reasons I'd picked Evergreen. Something about the surrounding forests had called to me.

"Delaney said you usually don't invite people over to your house."

Knox scowled at the road ahead. "Well, she's just a fount of knowledge, isn't she?"

I winced. It had to be hard to have people whisper behind your back so much. "Sorry."

His gaze flicked to me. "What do you have to be sorry for?"

"It has to be annoying to have people constantly talking about you."

"We're used to it. And she's right, anyway. We don't usually invite people back to our house."

A million questions flew through my mind, but I settled on the simplest of them all. "Why not?"

Knox's fingers tapped the steering wheel. "We're pretty private. We all get attention for different reasons. It's nice to have a place where we can just be ourselves. That can't happen if there are people coming over constantly."

My fingers dug into my thighs. "But you're taking me there."

"You're different."

Knox said it as though it were an undeniable truth.

"Different how?" I asked.

He cast me a quick smile. "You belong with us."

A riot of emotions took flight in my chest. I so badly wanted that to be true. "I'm not sure Easton feels that way."

Knox's scowl was back. "Easton's just a cranky fucker."

"Mr. Grumpy Cat."

He barked out a laugh. "Mr. Grumpy Cat."

Knox turned onto a gravel road flanked by towering redwoods. It had a beautiful, tunnel-like effect. Almost like a cocoon.

"I can see why you like living out here."

He glanced my way. "You like it?"

I nodded. "Feels safe."

"Good," he grunted.

Before long, Knox pulled to a stop at a massive gate. I'd never seen anything like it. It was a mixture of dark wood and gold metal. There were whimsical creatures woven throughout the design.

"That's beautiful."

Knox rolled down his window and punched in a code. "Cillian had it made. He's particular about design."

"You haven't really told me who Cillian is."

The gates opened, and Knox eased off the brake. "He's another friend. More like our big brother. He's the oldest and kind of the de facto leader."

"If you're all friends, shouldn't no one be the leader?" I asked.

Knox grinned. "Tell Cillian that."

He eased the SUV around several bends in the road until the forest parted and a structure came into view.

There was only one thing I could do.

Gasp.

CHAPTER TWENTY-ONE

Hayden

I'D NEVER SEEN ANYTHING LIKE THE IMAGE IN FRONT OF ME. *House* would've been the wrong word. Mansion wasn't right either. It honestly felt like a modern mountain castle.

The structure was massive. It had to be at least four floors, possibly five. It was a mixture of dark wood, stone, and glass. So much glass that you could see completely through the house in places. It made the home feel as if it were a part of the surrounding landscape.

"You live *here*?" I squeaked.

Knox slowed to a stop in front of the house, turning to face me. "Do you like it?"

There was worry in his voice, true concern that I might not like his home.

"It's stunning," I told him. "I've never seen anything like it."

A little of the tension bled out of Knox's shoulders. "Good. I'll give you the tour."

I nodded absently, sliding out of the SUV and staring at the enormous structure. It was definitely five stories.

Knox rounded the SUV, placed a palm at the small of my back, and guided me toward the house.

"How long have you lived here?" I asked.

"Almost four years now. Cillian designed the place from scratch and had it built in record time."

There was that enigmatic Cillian again. "It sounds like he has a real artist's eye."

Knox's lips twitched as he reached for the door handle. "He likes to be in control of every detail of everything. It only made sense that he'd want to design his home, too."

I frowned. "No one can be in control all the time." Life just didn't work out that way.

Knox shook his head. "Cill would argue that point."

I was starting to dread meeting this control freak friend of Knox's, if I was honest.

The moment we stepped into the grand foyer of the house, I was lifted off my feet. I let out a squeal of surprise as Cáel hugged me to him, nuzzling my neck. "Missed you," he grumbled.

I hugged him back. There was something about Cáel's lack of pretense, his honest authenticity, that I just loved. "Missed you, too."

He lowered me to the floor, gently brushing the hair out of my face. His fingers trailed down to the hood of my jacket, and he grinned.

I pinned him with a stare. "Did you leave the jackets on my bed?"

The grin widened, and he shrugged.

"It's too much, Cáel."

That grin morphed into a scowl. "You needed coats."

"Five of them?" I pressed.

Knox choked on a laugh behind me.

"And how did you get into my room?"

Cáel averted his gaze at that question.

"Jesus, Cáel. Rein it in," Easton muttered.

My gaze pulled to him. He stood, leaning against the wall.

He wore a maroon Henley with the sleeves pushed up, revealing muscular forearms. The dark-wash jeans he donned exposed bare feet. There was something so casual about those bare feet, almost intimate. As if I shouldn't be seeing the sight.

Easton's green eyes narrowed on me. "Hayden," he clipped.

"Grumpy Cat," I shot back.

His eyebrows flew toward his hairline. "What did you just call me?"

I met his stare dead on. "You look like that meme of the cat who's in a perpetual bad mood."

Easton's jaw worked back and forth. "I don't look like a *cat*."

"What's wrong with cats?" I challenged.

Knox started choking behind me.

Easton's gaze snapped to him. "You think this is funny?"

Knox couldn't hold in his laughter anymore. "Sorry, bro. She kind of has you pegged."

Easton let out a low growl, muttering something about *immature children* under his breath.

"That went well," I mumbled.

Cáel wrapped an arm around my shoulders, pulling me into his side. "Ignore him."

I wished I could. But no matter how much I told myself to forget about Easton, I couldn't seem to do it. He would pop into my mind at the most inconvenient moments. That just made me that much more annoyed by him.

"Let's give Hayden a tour of the downstairs before dinner," Knox suggested.

Cáel nodded, sending his blond braids and dreads swinging. My fingers itched to touch them, to know what they felt like against my skin. And the longer he held me pressed against him, the stronger the buzz ran through my muscles.

Knox started into a huge living room. The center of the space held a dark stone fireplace that disappeared into the impossibly high ceiling. It had a large wood mantel that housed an equally large television. There was a massive sectional that looked as if it could swallow me whole.

"You guys don't do small, do you?" I asked.

Cáel chuckled. "If you haven't noticed, we're on the larger side of things."

My cheeks heated. I had noticed. Perhaps a little too much.

Knox led us through the living space, pointing out different things and heading for a wide hallway. "We all have offices down here. Places where we can work and study. This is mine."

He flipped on a light, illuminating a gorgeous room. It, too, had its own fireplace, built-in bookshelves, a seating area, and a massive desk with a computer setup. The tall windows gave him a view of the backyard, including a massive pool.

"You have a pool? In the mountains?"

Knox grinned. "It's heated."

I just shook my head as he led us back into the hallway. "This is Maddox's office." He came up short. "Oh, hey, man. I didn't know you were in here."

Knox stepped to the side so that Maddox came into view behind his desk.

My mouth went dry as I took the man in. His dark, perfectly styled hair, his amber eyes. He was so stunning it almost hurt to look at him.

"Ms. Parrish," he greeted.

I swallowed. Did he want me to call him Professor Kavanaugh here, too? "Hello," I said, opting to leave names out altogether.

Knox sent him a warning look. "Don't be a prick, Mad. We aren't on campus."

Maddox simply stared back at Knox. "She's my *student*."

"So is Easton, and I don't hear you calling him *Mr. Gallagher*," Knox shot back.

"That's different, and you know it," Maddox growled.

I shifted, slipping out of Cáel's hold. "I'm sorry if my being here makes you uncomfortable. I can go—"

Cáel pulled me back to his side. "No." He glared at Maddox.

"Mad just has a stick up his ass that I'm going to help him remove if he's not careful," Knox gritted out.

I shook my head. "I get if he'd prefer not to have students in his home." I knew there were strict rules about teachers and staff having any sort of relationship with students.

"No one's going anywhere."

The voice that spoke was deeper than anyone else's in the room. It had a gritty rasp that sent shivers cascading over my skin.

My body was turning before I could tell it not to. And as it did, I froze, my mouth parting on a silent O.

I'd never seen a human being as large as the man in the massive doorway. He practically had to duck his head to make it inside. His eyes were a piercing green, darker than the twins'. His dark hair was buzzed close to his head. He had a lethal beauty I couldn't look away from.

But the freezing was instinct. Some part of my brain knew it because the man before me was a predator. And the way he was looking at me told me one thing.

I was the prey.

CHAPTER TWENTY-TWO

Cillian

THE SECOND HER SCENT TEASED MY NOSE, I WAS GONE. That mix of jasmine and fresh dew. So innocent. So pure. So mine.

My canines pressed against my gums, wanting to lengthen, wanting to bite. I needed to mark her so that the whole world knew she was mine.

Mine.

The single word was such a dangerous thought. Especially for someone as twisted as me. I knew that whomever my mate was wouldn't exactly be getting the best end of the deal.

They'd have to deal with my overbearing possessiveness. My obsessive protectiveness. My need to claim over and over again.

But it wasn't without reason. I had a list of enemies a mile long. And any of them would give their right arm to get their hands on someone important to me.

The fact that I'd spent the past few weeks dispatching one of the worst of my enemies, my father, didn't ease the feral panic coursing through me. There were too many others who would do anything to get to this woman.

Hayden.

My mouth curved silently around her name as I took her in.

Maddox had laid out the circumstances to me when he'd called. He'd been skeptical at first. An unprotected female dragon was beyond rare. The females of our kind had been slowly dying out, and many of them didn't have the ability to shift. But when Knox had called with the certainty that she was our mate, I'd been on the first plane out of Rhode Island and back to California.

Our mate.

And gods, was she beautiful. As she stood there, frozen in place, taking in my massive form, my beast roared in pleasure. He craved her submission. But my human half craved her trust.

She was tiny, almost fragile looking, at least compared to my own size. Her blonde hair curled around her shoulders in long waves. The sweater she wore hugged her curves in a way that had my dick straining against my zipper. But those eyes. Those violet eyes grabbed me by the throat and wouldn't let go.

"Hayden." My voice held an edge of a growl, but it couldn't be helped. My beast was battling for dominance, and I was doing everything I could to hold him back.

"Hi?"

She squeaked the word as if it were a question.

Cáel pulled her tighter into his side, sensing her uncertainty.

My eyes narrowed on him. No one would keep me from my mate, not even one of my brothers, one of my bond. I let my eyes flash in warning, telling Cáel exactly what would happen to him if he tried to intervene.

His eyes bled to silver in challenge.

I strode forward, extending a hand to Hayden. "I'm Cillian. Welcome to our home."

Hayden stared down at my palm as if it were a snake but finally extended her own hand to take mine.

The moment our skin touched, fire coursed through me. The burn was exquisite. Pleasure and pain in equal measure.

Mine, my beast roared.

The knowledge was so deep it was as if it were at the very core of my being, burned into my bones.

Hayden wavered on her feet, her pupils dilating. I moved in to steady her as Cáel held her up, glaring at me.

"Are you all right?" I did everything I could to gentle my voice. The last thing I wanted to do was terrify the poor girl.

She blinked up at me, her focus returning. "S-sorry. I keep doing that. I don't know what's wrong with me."

Of course, she didn't. Because Hayden had no idea what she was. Not a single clue.

But once we'd all touched her, she would be a ticking time bomb. There would only be so long that her dragon could lie dormant.

It happened sometimes, usually due to trauma, our inner beasts being shoved down. But being around others of our kind, especially our mate, would bring our dragons to the surface.

"Why don't we head to the dining room," I suggested. "We can get you something to eat and drink."

I held out my arm for Hayden to take.

Cáel's scowl deepened, and I bit back a grin. Jealous fool.

Hayden's hand trembled as it looped around my arm. But the moment she made contact, she seemed to melt into my side. My beast eased at her contact. I could only imagine what a nightmare he'd be when she left.

"So," I began, "you're from Seattle?"

She nodded. "Just outside the city."

"Knox said you grew up in foster care," I pressed.

Knox growled behind me as Hayden's eyes flared.

"Um, yes."

"Where did you live with your parents?"

I needed to know everything I could about Hayden if I was going to trace her lineage.

Those violet eyes narrowed. "Why does it matter?"

I gave a casual shrug. "Just making conversation. I'm curious."

"More like an interrogation," she muttered.

I bit back a laugh. Our girl had fire. Good. She'd need it. "It's okay, Little Flame. Plenty of time for me to find out everything about you."

Her pupils dilated at the promise in my voice, and my dick pressed harder against my zipper. She was my Little Flame, and even though I knew I was playing with fire, I kept right on going. I let her scent wrap around me, digging in so deep I knew I'd never get it out.

"What about you?" she challenged. "Where are you from?"

The depths of hell. That would've been closer to the truth. "Rhode Island."

"Oh," Hayden mumbled. "We lived in Maine."

Maine. Interesting. That would've been just beyond the reach of the horde I grew up in. A no-man's-land, really. There were few supernatural clans that far north. Mostly rogues who were looking to hide.

If her parents didn't trust the horde she'd been born into, their running would make sense. Because female dragons were rare. And once the supernatural world knew of Hayden's existence?

They would come for her.

CHAPTER TWENTY-THREE

Hayden

MY HANDS TREMBLED IN MY LAP AS I TOOK IN THE spread before me. How we were going to consume all this food, I had no idea. How I would eat a bite when I could feel five pairs of eyes studying me with a ravenous focus was another great question.

Knox reached under the table from his spot next to me and squeezed my leg. "Do you like steak?"

I nodded. I did. It was one of my favorite meals. But I wasn't sure how I was going to handle consuming it right now.

"Here," Cáel offered, loading my plate down with steak and all the side dishes. There were mashed potatoes, green bean casserole, salad, and garlic bread.

"That's too much," I protested.

He just shook his head. "You need to eat more."

I looked up, locking eyes with Maddox's amber ones. His expression was completely unreadable as he took me in.

"Mad, Hayden's pre-med," Knox began. "She wants to be a doctor."

There was a flicker of something I couldn't discern in those amber depths.

"A noble pursuit," Maddox said, taking a sip of red wine.

"You'll finally have someone to geek out with over all your science journals," Knox said with a grin.

I sat up straighter at that. "Which ones do you like?"

Maddox shifted slightly in his seat. "I have a particular interest in nanoscience and nanomedicine."

The first genuine smile spread across my face. "Interested in the treatment of cancer?"

His brows lifted in appreciation. "Yes. I am."

"God help us. No science talk at the dinner table," Easton grumbled from his seat next to Maddox.

The urge to stick my tongue out at him was so strong.

Cillian leaned back in his chair at the head of the table. "And what would you like to talk about?"

Easton's gaze shot to Cillian, his eyes going hot. "How about what an unbelievably moronic idea this is? One that's going to get us all killed?"

"East," Knox warned.

Easton's furious stare swept to Knox. "You *know*. Better than anyone what you're risking. You can't expect me to just sit by and watch."

Easton shoved back from the dining table and stalked out of the room.

"Not dramatic at all," Cillian muttered.

"Not helping, Cill," Maddox said quietly.

I looked around the table. What idea was going to get them all killed? I was starting to wonder if Fiona was right. Maybe these guys were mixed up in something I didn't want any part of.

Cillian turned his focus to me. "I apologize for our brother's behavior."

I swallowed hard. "It's not your fault. His actions are his own."

Cillian cut into his steak. "True, but he still put a damper on dinner."

I watched as Cillian crafted the perfect bite and popped it into his mouth. "What do you do, Cillian?"

He lifted his eyebrows in an amused question as he chewed.

"I mean, you look too old to be in college. I know Maddox is a professor."

Cillian leaned back in his chair and took a sip of wine. "I own a club. And a few other businesses."

My mind caught on the word *club*. That would be the perfect place to distribute drugs. Great, just great. I had found myself caught up in some cartel operation.

"What made you want to be a doctor?" he asked.

I picked at my meal. "I want to help people," I told him honestly.

"It's more than that," Cillian challenged.

I met his stare, refusing to back down. "Everyone has a story."

"And yours is?" he pressed.

"You haven't earned it yet."

Cillian's green eyes heated. "Little Flame…"

My belly dipped and rolled as I tried to remind myself that this man was likely a drug dealer.

Instead, I focused on my meal. I ate as quickly as possible, only answering questions when I absolutely had to. As soon as we were finished eating, I pushed back from the table. "I'm sorry. I really need to get back to the dorms so that I can get my homework done."

Maddox nodded, seeming relieved. "Of course. Knox will take you."

"You could study here," Cáel suggested hopefully.

I shook my head. "I don't have any of my books."

His shoulders slumped, and I felt instantly guilty. "Knox and I are going to study in the library this weekend if you want to join."

He brightened at that, nodding and pulling me into a hug. "Stay safe."

My muscles sang at the contact. "You, too."

He simply grunted.

Cillian watched me as if I were a puzzle and he was putting together the pieces. "See you soon, Hayden."

It felt like both a promise and a threat.

I made a noncommittal noise and headed for the door, hoping Knox would follow.

"Thank you for dinner," I called without looking back, grabbing my jacket on the way out.

The X5 beeped as I strode toward it, and I climbed inside.

Knox was quiet as we drove back to school, not even looking at me. By the time he parked in the quad, my stomach was in knots.

"I'm sorry about East," he said quietly.

I studied the man next to me. His typically easy-going expression had gone stormy, and I couldn't resist reaching for his hand.

"His actions aren't on you," I assured him.

Knox lifted his gaze to mine, so much pain there. "He's decided that all relationships are doomed."

I frowned. "He obviously has a relationship with all of you."

"Not those kinds of relationships, romantic ones."

"Oh." My mind spun with a million questions, but I kept coming back to one. "Why?"

Knox was quiet for a long moment, and then he spoke. "Our brother was married. So in love. I've never seen another person happier."

Dread pooled in my belly.

"Ryan's wife was murdered, and he fell apart. Kept devolving until he wasn't our brother anymore. He was a stranger." Knox's fingers flexed around mine. "He killed our entire family and burned the house down around them. East and I barely made it out alive. Ryan let himself burn with them."

My throat was on fire, agony ripping through it. I could feel Knox's pain as if it were my own. And maybe it was. Our stories were different but far too similar.

So, I did the only thing I could. I unbuckled my seat belt and climbed into his lap.

I wrapped my arms around Knox as if I could take all his pain. "I'm so sorry." I nuzzled his neck. "You aren't alone."

It was the only thing I wanted to know when I was in the depths of my grief, that someone was with me.

Knox pulled back a fraction so that his eyes locked with mine. "I'm not, am I?"

"No," I whispered.

His head dipped, so slowly, giving me all the time I'd need to move. But I didn't.

The moment Knox's mouth connected with mine, fire burst free in my veins. An inferno of heat and need and sensation. I pressed closer to him, needing more, needing everything.

Knox took and took, teasing a moan free from my lips as his tongue stroked mine.

My fingers twisted in his shirt, pulling him harder against me. My core tightened in desperate need. And it felt like invisible wings beat against my rib cage.

Knox tore his mouth away from mine, his breathing ragged and eyes burning gold.

My fingers flew to my lips. They still burned.

And some part of me knew that nothing would ever be the same.

Chapter Twenty-Four

Easton

The whiskey burned as I shot it down my throat. The fiery pain was exactly what I needed. Anything to distract me from the agony that was *her*.

My twin just *had* to invite her here, into our sanctuary. And now her scent was everywhere. That dewy jasmine. So pure. So naïve.

It had seeped into everything. The furniture. The carpets. The fucking walls.

There was no getting Hayden out now. She was all around me.

The call of her was so strong. As if my beast could already feel her just because my brothers had touched her, because they had begun the mating process.

It was a long way from being cemented. That would take the actual bite to complete. Something I'd never do. But I didn't know where that would lead me. Possibly going out of my mind with want and need.

I grabbed the bottle of whiskey to refill my shot glass, but a hand wrapped around it, pulling it from my grasp.

Cillian glared at me with those dark green alpha eyes. We were the only ones in our small horde that could meet his stare, but there was still a pressure to his gaze.

"You think this is going to solve your problems?" he growled.

I shrugged, releasing my hold on the bottle as Maddox and Cáel filed into the room. "It's better than pretending everything is all sunshine and fucking rainbows."

Cáel's expression darkened. "She's our mate. It's a gift. You know how rare this is."

Rare was an understatement. The number of female dragons had dropped to an alarming number. Finding a true mate bond was practically impossible. Most dragon males ended up mating another type of shifter or even a human.

I reached for a different bottle of whiskey behind the bar. This was Cillian's good shit. I poured it into the glass and shot it back. "You guys have at it."

Cillian set his bottle on the bar. "You know it doesn't work that way."

It didn't. No matter what, I would feel her. Once they fully bonded with her, it would be pure torture, not that it wasn't already. Hayden was already haunting my dreams. I didn't want to think about how bad it would be tonight with her scent everywhere.

My gaze flicked to Maddox. "It's not like you're all that thrilled about this either."

He sent me one of those damned teacher stares. Like he was disappointed in me. "I'll never see Hayden as anything but a gift. The fact that I need to keep my distance from her for the next four years doesn't change that."

Cillian grunted. "Good luck with that."

Maddox's jaw hardened. "She's young, Cill. A good thirteen years younger than us. Innocent. Has no idea this world even exists. You need to remember that."

The green in Cillian's eyes swirled, deepening until it was almost black.

Cáel was usually the one to scare the shit out of me, but when Cillian actually lost it, he was terrifying.

"She's my mate." Cillian's words were so low they were barely audible, but they vibrated with his fury.

Cáel muttered a curse, moving so that he could easily dive between Cillian and Maddox. If Cill actually lost it, Cáel would be toast.

Maddox remained casually calm. That was his gift, staying at ease no matter what shit flew our way. From the dragon council to rival hordes. He never showed a flicker of panic.

"I'm not saying you can't have her," Maddox began. The words eased the slightest amount of tension in Cillian. "I'm just saying that you need to move slowly." He looked around the room. "You all do."

My back teeth ground together. "I'm not moving at all."

Maybe distance was what I needed. Space to get this pull under control. I could go roaming. Maybe go stay with Cillian's half brothers in Rhode Island. He'd said they were good people.

But some small part of me knew that even an entire country between us wouldn't dull Hayden's siren song. Because that was exactly what she was. Some mystical creature who was going to bring destruction to all of us.

Cáel glanced at Cillian. "Who do you have guarding her?"

"James and Sean." Cillian cracked his neck as if to relieve some invisible pressure there.

But I knew what the pressure was. Now that he'd touched Hayden, the mating urge would be riding him hard. The *need* to claim Hayden. But also the need to keep her safe, protected.

It was no surprise that Cillian had put two of his best enforcers on Hayden duty. It was a miracle he'd even let her leave horde lands.

"And what happens when she realizes two hulking dudes are following her everywhere?" I challenged.

Cillian's eyes flashed in my direction. "They know how not to be seen."

They were good, I'd give him that, but they couldn't stay hidden forever. Especially not on campus.

"This is such a fucking moronic idea," I spat.

Knox's eyes bled to gold as he strode into the room. "You've made your opinion *abundantly* clear. So much so that you made Hayden feel uncomfortable in our home, in *her* home."

Those two words, *her home*, had me seeing red. "You don't get to decide that. Unless someone died and made you alpha," I snarled.

Knox's chest rose and fell in ragged pants as his nostrils flared. "You need to pull your head out of your ass and do it now. I won't lose her because you're scared."

Claws pierced the skin on my fingers as I struggled to hold back my shift. "I'm not *scared*. I'm smart. I'm not going to let anyone hold the keys to my sanity. Not ever. I can't believe you would either. Especially just for a piece of ass."

It was the wrong thing to say.

There was no warning; Knox simply charged. He hit me in a football tackle, sending me flying backward. We rolled, each of us landing blows to each other's ribs, jaws, and who knew where else.

Hands latched on to my shirt, jerking me out of the tumble.

"Enough!" Cillian yelled, the alpha vibes filling his tone and forcing my head down in submission. "Being at odds like this is the last thing we need. We have to be at the top of our game, or we could lose Hayden altogether. Because once the supernatural world finds out she's a dragon, they will come for her. And they won't hesitate to slaughter us to get to her."

CHAPTER TWENTY-FIVE

Hayden

I SAT BACK ON MY BED TO SLIP ON MY VANS. EVERYTHING HURT. My throat burned. My muscles ached. And I was pretty sure I was running a fever.

My bed called to me. It would be so easy to just slip beneath the covers and fall back asleep. But I couldn't. I wasn't going to miss classes this early in the semester.

"What's wrong with you?" Delaney asked, her nose wrinkling.

I swallowed against the pain in my throat. "I'm not feeling that great."

She took a giant step back. "Well, stay away from me. I have big plans tomorrow."

Gee, thanks for the sensitivity.

Delaney bounced on the balls of her feet. "We're going to *Ashes & Emeralds*." Her voice went shrill on the name.

"Ashes & Emeralds?"

She grinned. "It's this *amazing* club. Maggie's getting us all fake IDs so we can get in." Her smile dropped a bit. "But not if you give me the bubonic plague."

The idea of traipsing to a club right now was about as likely as me running two marathons back-to-back. No, thank you. "Have fun," I mumbled.

Her face scrunched as she took me in. "Maybe you should go to the health center."

It wasn't a bad idea. Between my almost-fainting spells and now this, I probably should get checked out. "I'll go after my morning classes."

"Just try not to infect anyone," Delaney mumbled as she grabbed her bag and headed out the door.

That was as warm and fuzzy as I was going to get from my roomie.

I pushed to my feet, the world swimming around me. *Crap.* I took a second to get my sea legs and then pulled on my backpack.

It took me far longer than it should've to make it out of the dorm. By the time I got outside, I was out of breath. That definitely wasn't normal.

Each step I took felt like my legs weighed one hundred pounds each. Students sent me puzzled looks as I passed. I was sure I looked like shit. *Great.* Just more of an epic first impression in my new world.

I made my way slowly across campus, and by the time I arrived at the science building, I felt like I'd crawled a marathon in the desert. My mouth felt as if it might crack, it was so dry. My muscles trembled and ached. And I was burning up.

As I stepped inside, I came up short, almost running into Professor Brent.

He frowned down at me. "Hayden?"

"Hello, Professor," I croaked.

His brows pinched. "Are you ill?"

"I'm feeling a little under the weather."

Brent took a step back. "You should go to the health center."

"I'm going right after my class."

He studied me for a minute, something working behind those

hazel eyes. "I do admire your dedication to your studies. Feel free to lie down on the couch in my office if you need a break today."

A shiver wracked through me, and it had nothing to do with the fever I was rocking. "Thank you," I whispered.

He nodded. "And don't forget to email me to set up our meeting."

I made a noncommittal sound and gave him a nod as I pushed into the sea of students. They were blurry around the edges, as if each one was fading in and out. Maybe something was really wrong with me.

My feet were sluggish, tripping over each other as I moved through the halls. One caught on my heel, and I started to stumble.

Strong hands caught me. "Careful, Ms. Parrish."

My eyes lifted to warm amber ones. The moment our gazes connected, concern filled Maddox's expression.

"What's wrong?"

"I don't feel so good," I rasped.

That concern morphed into panic as Maddox wrapped an arm around my waist. He guided me down the hall, taking all my weight easily. "Come on."

I went willingly. I wouldn't have been able to fight him if I'd tried. It now felt almost like someone had drugged me.

Maddox led me into his office, shutting the door behind us and guiding me to a leather couch. He eased me onto the sofa, slipping off my backpack. "Tell me what's wrong."

I blinked a few times, trying to bring him back into focus, but it was no use. "My throat. And my body hurts. I think I have a fever."

My voice didn't sound like my own. It was far away and had a gritty rasp.

Maddox cursed, pulling out his phone and tapping the screen before he pressed it to his ear. "You need to get to my office right fucking now." There was a pause. "Yes, it's about Hayden. And you'll be lucky if I don't skin you myself."

My mouth pulled down in a frown. Who was he talking to?

The thought passed quickly because everything hurt so badly. I began to list to the side, and Maddox caught me with another muttered curse.

"Easy, *Mo Ghràidh*. You'll be okay."

I leaned into Maddox, his scent wrapping around me. It was a smoky, burnt orange. It had a bite to it just like the man himself.

"What's wrong with me?"

"Nothing's wrong with you," he whispered.

I whimpered. "Hurts."

Maddox cursed again, but then his hand slipped under my hair, and he began kneading my neck.

The moment his skin touched mine, the pain eased a fraction. It wasn't gone, but the worst of it faded. That drugged feeling stayed, though. Darkness pulled at me.

"Just breathe, *Mo Ghràidh*. Just breathe. It will pass."

"What...will?" My words were slow, sluggish, as if I could barely get them past my lips.

"The pain. I'll take it away."

And he did.

CHAPTER TWENTY-SIX

Knox

M Y TIRES SQUEALED AS I FLEW INTO A PARKING SPOT behind the science building. This lot was supposed to be for faculty only, but I didn't give a damn. They could ticket me if they wanted to.

All I could think about was getting to Hayden. A million different what-ifs flew through my mind. Each one was worse than before.

I jumped out of the driver's seat, slammed my door behind me, and took off for the back door. I struggled to keep my inhuman speed under control. If I revealed how fast I could truly move, I'd get locked up in some government facility for sure.

Battling against my beast's instincts, I jerked the door open and stalked down the hallway. It was mostly empty now, but I still didn't risk my increased speed. I jogged like a human would toward Maddox's office.

I'd heard the fury beneath his words. Something had happened. Something bad. Something he blamed me for.

My gut twisted as I picked up my speed.

It only took a matter of seconds for me to reach his closed

door. I didn't bother knocking; I simply jerked it open. Storming inside, I came up short.

Hayden lay against Maddox. Her skin was far too pale, but her cheeks were flushed. Her eyes were closed as if she were sleeping, but that made no sense.

"Close. The. Door," Maddox growled.

I quickly obeyed. "What's wrong with her? Is she sick? Do we need to get her to a healer?"

Maddox's eyes flashed gold. "Did you touch her?"

I stilled. "Sure, I—"

"Did you *touch* her?" he snarled.

Oh, shit.

My spine jerked straight. "We kissed," I admitted, panic coursing through me.

Maddox let out a stream of curses. "What were you thinking? You've tethered her to us without her permission."

I'd heard about this kind of thing happening with true mates, but I didn't think it was really possible. "It just happened."

His eyes flashed again. "What? You tripped, fell, and landed on her mouth?"

My back teeth ground together. "No. I was upset about East. She was comforting me. And it just happened."

"It didn't just *happen*. You let it happen," Maddox snapped. "And now everything will change. She'll need touch from us. If she doesn't get it for too long, she'll get sick."

My gut churned. *Shit.* This was my fault. "I'm sorry—I didn't think it would happen like this."

"No. You didn't think at all," Maddox challenged.

He was right. I'd been selfish and short-sighted. But Hayden's pull was too strong to resist. Maybe that made me weak, but I'd always be weak for her.

"What do I do?" I asked softly.

"Right now, you need to get her home. Get East or Cáel to drive. You stay in the back with her. She needs skin-to-skin contact.

In a few hours, she should feel better. But from now on, if she goes more than ten or so hours without contact from one of us, she'll start to get sick."

A lead weight settled somewhere deep. How the hell were we going to manage that? I'd just have to find a way.

"How long does it last?" I asked.

Maddox's jaw worked back and forth. "Until the bond is complete."

But once the bond was completed, there would be a new risk. Hayden would most likely go into her first dragon heat. There were many legends about what that would entail. Bonds would be locked up for days on end, trying to satiate their mate who had an endless need coursing through her.

I swallowed hard. "I'll make sure this doesn't happen again."

Maddox pinned me with his stare. "Yes, you will."

He looked down at Hayden. The blonde strands fluttered around her face as she breathed deeply. There was so much adoration in his gaze, so much care and protectiveness and devotion. It didn't matter that Maddox was holding himself back from Hayden. He was already gone for her.

I pulled out my phone and typed out a text to Easton.

> **Me:** *Meet me in the parking lot behind the science building now.*

It didn't matter that we'd come to blows just last night. I knew that he would always be there for me when I needed him.

> **East:** *On my way.*

I crossed to the couch, grabbing Hayden's backpack. I frowned at the broken zipper as I put it on. Bending, I reached for Hayden.

Maddox's hand flexed around her waist as if it were a battle to let her go. But finally, he relented, and I lifted her into my arms.

Hayden whimpered in pain, and guilt sliced into me. I shifted my hand so that it slid under her shirt, my palm against her back.

Her skin was burning up, and that guilt dug deeper. I'd done this to her, caused her pain.

"Come on," Maddox bit out, getting to his feet. "If anyone asks, she has the flu. You're taking her to the doctor."

I jerked my head in a nod as he opened the door.

We filed out into the hallway, making our way to the back door. Between my beast's strength and how tiny Hayden was, she felt like nothing in my arms. But that only drove home her vulnerability. She was fragile, and I had to remember that.

Maddox held open the back door, and I stepped out into the sunshine.

Easton pushed off my SUV, his gaze narrowing on us. I saw the panic flare in his green eyes, the sheer terror as he strode toward us. "What happened?"

"Mating fever," Maddox muttered.

Easton's gaze jerked to me. "What did you do?"

I bit the inside of my cheek. "I fucked up, okay? I know it. Will you just help me get her back to our house?"

So many emotions played over Easton's face, but terror was at the root of all of them. And I'd put that there. Because I'd bound Hayden to us before anyone was ready, before any of us were prepared.

Easton's gaze locked with mine. "You've changed everything."

I swallowed hard. "I know."

"Cillian's going to have your ass."

I knew that, too. There would be consequences for what I'd done. But looking down at the woman in my arms, she was the only thing I could think about. She was everything. And I'd do whatever it took to keep her safe.

CHAPTER TWENTY-SEVEN

Hayden

A COCOON OF WARMTH SURROUNDED ME—THAT, AND a familiar scent. Pine and rain. Together, it felt like a home I hadn't had in years. I burrowed deeper and let out a little moan.

Arms tightened around me, and I froze.

Arms?

My eyes flew open, meeting familiar green ones with gold flecks. Those golden particles were in a pattern that only belonged to Knox.

"What—?" My question cut off because I wasn't exactly sure what it was I wanted to ask.

My gaze jumped around the room. I was lying in a massive bed, one that was larger than a king. A thick, white comforter was pulled around us. The walls of the room were dark teal, but color-ful art adorned them, bringing Knox's personality into the space.

"What happened?" I croaked.

Knox reached for a cup on the nightstand. "Here, take a sip."

My hand trembled as I took it. The moment the cool water touched my throat, I gulped it down. It was heaven.

When I'd drained the glass dry, I handed it back to him, a million questions in my eyes.

"We think you had a twenty-four-hour flu," he explained.

My eyes went wide. "How long have I been here?"

Knox winced. "Almost that long. You ran into Maddox yesterday morning and were super out of it, so he called me."

Now it was my turn to wince. Maddox already wanted nothing to do with me. I could only imagine how he felt now.

"And you brought me here?" I asked.

Knox nodded. "I didn't want you in the dorms. You needed quiet to rest."

"And this is your room…"

It wasn't exactly a question, but he explained anyway. "Yeah. You've been sleeping for pretty much the entire last day."

I jerked upright at that. "My classes. The diner."

Knox tried to make me lie back against the pillows. "Don't worry. Mad emailed all your professors, and Cillian called Fiona. You're covered."

I glanced at the clock on the nightstand. "I can still make my shift at the diner today—"

"Oh, no," Knox said, expression going hard. "You need to rest."

"Knox—"

The door to his bedroom opened, and Cáel's massive form filled the entryway. His light blue eyes widened. "You're awake." He turned to glare at Knox. "Why didn't you call me?"

Knox rolled his eyes. "She *just* woke up."

Cáel bared his teeth at Knox. "You still should've called."

He strode toward the bed, carrying a tray, and set it on the nightstand closest to me. He sat on the edge of the bed, his hands immediately going to my face. The touch was painfully gentle as he tested my forehead and cheeks.

"How do you feel?"

I thought about it for a moment. I remembered how awful I'd felt yesterday. There was none of that now. I felt…remarkably good. "I feel completely fine."

My stomach rumbled as if to punctuate the point.

My cheeks flushed, and I ducked my head.

Cáel chuckled. "You need to eat."

My stomach squeezed as if to agree with him, and Cáel lifted the tray onto the bed.

"Start with soup, just in case," Knox said.

Cáel sent Knox another glare.

I looked between the two of them as I took the bowl of what looked like chicken soup. "Are you two in a fight?"

Redness crept up Knox's throat, and Cáel grunted.

"I'm going to take that as a yes." I studied them both as I lifted a bite of the soup to my lips. My eyes closed as the flavors played on my tongue. I couldn't help it, I moaned. "This is the best thing I've ever tasted."

When my eyes opened, I found two sets pinned on my mouth. "What?"

Knox shook himself out of his stupor. "I'm glad it's good. Then you'll eat it all."

I fought the urge to stick my tongue out at him.

"There's fresh bread, too," Cáel said, pushing a plate closer to me.

It smelled amazing. "Who cooks?"

They shared a look.

"What?"

Knox shifted in his spot on the bed. "We have a cook."

Of course, they did. Must be nice to be rolling in cash. The thought had me biting my lip, my earlier worries about some sort of drug-dealing operation flaring to life.

Footsteps sounded in the hallway, and I looked up to see Cillian stride into the room.

My spoon froze in midair, and my mouth went dry.

He looked absolutely lethal in his black suit that was tailored perfectly to his body. He wore a black shirt beneath it with a couple of buttons undone. He was some dark, avenging angel, and his eyes were locked on me.

"Hayden."

Cillian's voice was pure grit. Low and coated in sandpaper and promise.

"Hi," I squeaked.

He strode toward the bed, his eyes flashing at Knox for the barest moment before returning to me. But I'd seen the warning there. Why was everyone pissed at Knox? Did they not want me here? Maybe they were worried I'd get everyone sick.

"I can go home," I said quickly.

Cillian's teeth ground together. "You aren't going anywhere, Little Flame."

My stomach hollowed out at that.

"I have to go to work in a little bit."

Annoyance flashed in his eyes. "Fiona doesn't need you today."

I sat up, meeting his gaze in challenge. "Since I'm scheduled to work, I'm guessing she does."

Cillian let out a low growl. "You've been sick. You need to rest."

"I feel completely fine. No fever. It was just a twenty-four-hour bug like Knox said."

Cillian's gaze prowled toward Knox. "Is that what he said?"

Knox winced, staying silent.

Cillian's gaze stayed locked on him. "Weren't you going to help Easton with yard work?"

Knox's mouth opened as if to argue, and then he snapped it closed again. He nodded, pushing up from the bed. "I'll call you later to check on you."

My brows pulled together. He was leaving me to do *yard work*? What the heck?

I watched Knox stalk out of the room, staring even after he'd disappeared.

"Eat, Little Flame," Cillian commanded.

My gaze flicked to him. "You're very pushy. You know that, right?"

Cáel choked on a laugh.

Cillian's lips twitched. I'd never seen him smile, but just the flicker of it was devastating.

He lowered himself to the bed, tracing an invisible pattern with his long fingers on the duvet. "I'm used to getting my way."

"I bet," I mumbled as I took another bite of soup. "I'm not eating because you told me to. I'm eating because this soup is amazing."

Cáel grinned at me. It was that rusty, feral smile. "I'll bring you more for lunch tomorrow."

I wouldn't argue with that. The cafeteria overwhelmed me. Eating alone at one of the outdoor tables was much more my speed.

"Thanks," I mumbled, hurrying to finish the soup.

I dropped my spoon into the empty bowl. "I really do need to get to work." I glanced down at myself, noticing for the first time that I was wearing what looked like Knox's sweats. My cheeks heated. "Do you know where my clothes are?"

Cáel inclined his head toward the couch on the opposite wall. There was a pile of neatly folded clothes. "We had them washed. But I really think you need to rest—"

I pushed up and kissed his cheek. "Thank you. Would you be able to drive me to town? I could get an Uber—"

A low growl sounded from my other side. "Hayden…"

I stood, crossing to my clothes. "I'm fine, Cillian. I swear. And I'm not missing a shift. I can get an Uber if it's a pain for Cáel to take me—"

"I'll drive you."

I stilled at Cillian's words, my palms going clammy.

A fifteen-minute car ride alone with a possible drug-dealing male model who turned me inside out? What could go wrong?

Chapter Twenty-Eight

Hayden

I scanned the front yard, looking for Knox, but there was no one. I turned to look through the massive windows, and there was no one in the backyard either. Tipping my head back, I peeked up at Cáel. "I thought Knox had to help with some yard work."

Cáel shifted, a backpack looking comically tiny on his massive frame. "Somewhere else on the property."

"How big is this place?"

He sent me a sheepish smile. "We've got almost a thousand acres."

My eyes bugged. "Like a one and three zeros thousand?"

He nodded.

I bit my lip as I heard the low rumble of an engine. Those thoughts of drug dealing filled my mind again. "Am I safe with Cillian?" I whispered.

Cáel moved in then, wrapped his arms around me, and bent to nuzzle my neck. He breathed me in, his body shuddering with the action. "I would never let you go with anyone you weren't safe with."

It was slightly ironic that I was asking the person most people on campus were absolutely terrified of. But Cáel had never made me feel anything but completely safe. Cillian, on the other hand, set my nerves on edge. It wasn't a bad feeling exactly, but there was an underlying energy that told me a predator was nearby.

The rumbling purr of an engine grew louder, and a sleek, black sports car rounded the curve of the house. The vehicle looked more like it belonged on a racetrack than on regular roads. But here it was.

Cáel released his hold on me and moved to the car, opening the door. He dropped the backpack inside.

I frowned. "That's not mine." My backpack was the gray one with the mangled zipper.

Cáel shook his head. "Knox got you a new one. The zipper was busted on yours."

My mouth pressed into a firm line. "It still worked."

He crossed to me, his lips brushing featherlight across my temple. "Let us take care of you."

My body came alive at the barest touch. Nerve-endings zinged, and my skin tingled.

Guilt swamped me. Just two days ago, I'd been in Knox's lap, *kissing* him. I shouldn't be feeling this way about someone he considered a brother. I shouldn't be feeling this way about any of the men in this house if I was smart.

I swallowed hard as Cáel moved out of the way. Crossing to the vehicle, I lowered myself inside. I'd been right about it being meant for the racetrack. The interior looked more like a spaceship than a car.

Cáel shut the door behind me, and I couldn't help my slight jump.

Cillian's lips twitched, and I glared at him.

"What is this thing, anyway?" I clipped.

The engine revved as if in response. "This *thing* is one of the best cars on the planet. The Hennessey Venom F5."

Venom sounded like an appropriate car for Cillian. Because

127

if there was one thing that was obvious about this man, it was that he was lethal.

My gaze tracked over him as he drove us toward the property's exit. My focus landed on his hands. There were no tattoos there like on Cáel's hands, but there were patterns of a sort.

Scars littered his knuckles and the backs of his hands. Some looked deep and wide, but others were thin, as if the flesh had simply split open and then miraculously healed.

"You're staring, Little Flame."

I jolted at his deep voice, my gaze snapping back to the road as we passed through the ornate gates. "What happened to your hands?"

From the corner of my eye, I could see his fingers tighten on the wheel.

"Was on my own young. Had to find a way to make money."

I frowned. "A way that left scars?"

Cillian turned onto the road that led into town. "I was always a good fighter. You have to be if you're living on the streets. I just let myself earn money for it."

My stomach bottomed out. "Underground fights?"

There'd been a boy who'd come through my foster home who'd gotten involved in one of those. It was brutal, and there were usually organized crime entities involved. One time, he'd been hurt so badly that he'd ended up in the hospital.

Cillian gave the slightest lift of his chin in acknowledgment. "Wasn't that bad."

It was a lie. His body told me as much.

"I'm sorry you had to do that," I whispered.

"Such a tender heart, my Little Flame."

My gaze flicked to Cillian as he slowed at a light. Our eyes locked, and I was frozen there. I swore I could feel his heartbeat pulsing against my own.

He let out a low growl, jerking his gaze away from me and taking his foot off the brake.

What the hell was that?

Something was very, very wrong with me. I rarely had crushes. The one time I'd let myself, it had ended in disaster. So, I kept my head down and stayed focused on my studies. But now, it was like each of these men had a gravitational pull.

I tried my best to shake it off as Cillian pulled to a stop in front of Spark's. I moved to open the door, but Cillian grabbed my hand.

The contact was gentle, but it sent a wave of heat coursing through me.

"Promise me you'll take it easy today."

I swallowed hard as I looked into those dark green eyes. "I will."

Cillian's jaw worked back and forth. "I put my number in your phone. Call me if you need *anything*."

My mouth went dry. "Okay."

He released me, and the moment his touch was gone, I missed it like a limb.

I climbed out of the car and hurried into the diner, practically running Fiona over as I headed for the staff room.

Her eyes widened. "I thought you were sick."

"Just a twenty-four-hour bug. I'm feeling much better."

"You sure?" she pressed.

I nodded quickly. "Yup. Just let me know where you want me."

"All right. You can take tables one through eight."

"Thanks." I hurried into the staff room, deposited my backpack in my locker, and donned my apron. Then I headed out onto the floor.

I got lost in my routine, taking orders and clearing tables. As I came to a stop next to one table, a weight settled in my stomach.

"Hayden," Professor Brent greeted, his gaze sweeping over me. "I'd heard you were ill."

I gripped my order pad a little tighter. "Just a twenty-four-hour thing. I'll be back in class tomorrow."

"Glad to hear it." His gaze kept roaming. "I didn't know you worked here."

"Yup. After school." That much was obvious, but I wasn't sure what else to say. "Do you know what you'd like to order?"

Brent leaned forward into my personal space. "What do *you* like?"

Nausea swept through me, and I took a step back. "The cheeseburger's really good."

He grinned. "Then I'll take that. Medium. And a Coke."

"I'll get that right in for you."

I turned on my heel and headed to give the order to Ian, but I could feel Brent's eyes on me. Everything in me was screaming in alert. I was safe. There were a dozen people in the diner right now.

While I waited for the order to come up, I rolled silverware, listening to two burly guys talk about an upcoming football game. Their chatter was calming, normal. Then the bell dinged.

"Order up," Ian called.

I turned to check, and it was Professor Brent's. Steeling myself, I took the plate and headed for his table.

His gaze locked on me as I walked toward him. With each step, my heart beat a little faster.

I forced a smile. "Here you go, Professor."

I set the plate down and moved to quickly back up, but I wasn't fast enough.

Brent caught my arm. His hold wasn't painful, but it wasn't loose either. "Thank you, Hayden. When we're not on campus, you can call me Paul. I'd like us to be friends."

Sweat gathered along my spine as panic began to set in. How the hell did I answer that?

"Hey, Hayden," a loud, booming voice called across the restaurant.

At the sound, Brent's hand dropped away, and a whoosh of air left my lungs.

I quickly turned toward the voice. It was one of the men at the counter. One of the football guys. I had no idea how he knew my name, but I was grateful. I headed right in his direction to see what he needed.

But I knew I'd have to face Professor Brent eventually, and dread settled in deep at the thought.

CHAPTER TWENTY-NINE

Hayden

I SIGHED AS I DROPPED MY FANCY NEW BACKPACK ON THE chair in my room. It had been a week. Between trying to avoid Professor Creeper, a mountain of schoolwork, and Knox acting all sorts of weird, I was exhausted.

It wasn't just Knox behaving strangely. It was all the guys, except for Cáel. Knox would show up each morning with hot chocolate and breakfast. He'd kiss my forehead and then immediately step back as if I had some communicable disease. He'd keep a foot of distance between us at all times after that.

Easton just kept his distance in general, unless he was glaring at me in one of our two shared classes. Maddox only ever called me Ms. Parrish, and when he did, he never made eye contact. Cillian texted occasionally but only to ask how I was feeling.

Thank God there was Cáel. He and I had taken to late-night study sessions in the library together. He'd walk me back to my dorm each night, wrapping me in a hug so tender it would make me want to cry. Then he'd kiss me on the temple and say goodnight.

But even with his kindness, I was left completely and utterly confused. What did any of them want? I was beyond tired of all the second-guessing.

Maggie grinned at me as she crossed the small room and dropped something credit card sized on my desk. "You're coming with us this time."

My brows pulled together as I took in the nicer one of Delaney's friends. "Coming with you?"

Delaney scowled at me. "Not dressed like that, she's not."

I picked up the tiny object. It was the same photo that was on my student ID, but this one read *The State of Wyoming* and had a different name and birthday.

I turned to face Maggie. "What is this?"

She rolled her eyes. "Don't you want to have a little more of a life than living in the library?"

My cheeks burned. "I have to get good grades to keep my scholarship."

"And is going out one night going to stop that?"

No, it wouldn't. The truth was, with all my study time with Cáel, I was ahead in most of my classes. I stared down at the ID.

"She doesn't want to go," Delaney snapped. "Leave the nerd here."

"Come on, Hayden," Maggie pushed. "Live a little. You can invite Knox and Cáel, too, if you want."

There it was, the real reason for the invite.

"I'd rather not," I grumbled.

Delaney's eyes brightened. "Trouble in paradise?"

"I could just use a break."

Maggie grinned. "Then this is the perfect plan. Maybe you'll meet someone new."

I bet she and Delaney would just love that. But as I stared down at the ID, I realized I wanted to go. To have one of those quintessential college experiences.

I dropped the ID onto my desk. "What should I wear?"

Maggie's smile widened. "Why don't you come shopping in my closet."

⁓

I *never* should've let Maggie dress me. I tugged on the black spandex miniskirt that barely covered my ass. She'd paired it with these ripped-up tights and boots that came to mid-thigh. From the front, the black shirt she'd given me didn't look that risqué, but when I turned around, I realized there was no back.

Dumb. Dumb. Dumb.

My feet already ached from the boots I was wearing, and we'd barely walked a block from where the Uber had dropped us off. Maggie and Bella had linked arms and were chattering away. They were dressed in outfits similar to mine, so at least I wasn't alone.

I glanced at Delaney, who was wearing a skin-tight black minidress with a million little cutouts all over it. "Are you sure this is the right place?"

From what I could tell, we were in the middle of nowhere. It looked more like an industrial park than somewhere a club might be.

Her white teeth flashed as she smiled. "We came last week when you were sick. It's the best place around. You're gonna freak."

My stomach twisted. I didn't know if freaking out was a state I wanted to voluntarily be in. I should've gone to the library with Cáel.

Letting out a whoosh of air, I picked up my pace. The gravel made it twice as hard to walk in these damned boots. As we turned a corner, the faint hum of noise tickled my ears, and a prickle of awareness hummed across my skin as if a phantom energy had swept across me.

As the building came into view, I gasped. It wasn't the structure itself. That looked like the rest of the buildings we'd passed, a mixture of metal and brick. It was the massive line that wrapped around it that had me gaping.

Too many people to count. Most of them made our outfits look tame. One woman wore a completely see-through dress with no bra and simply a thong underneath. But I had to admit, she looked stunning. And I admired her fearlessness.

"We'll be waiting here all night," I muttered, trying to do the math in my head for how long it would take us to get inside.

"Please," Delaney said, waving me off and heading directly for the front door.

A massive man with tattoos and a clipboard grinned as she walked toward him. "D-money. Back again?"

She smiled flirtatiously. "Cal, got room for four more?"

"For you? Always." He lifted the velvet rope and let us inside.

Delaney stretched up on her tiptoes and pressed a kiss to his cheek. I also saw the flash of a hundred-dollar bill she slid into his pocket. "You're the best."

This was so far out of my league, it wasn't funny.

A second bouncer held up his hand for us to wait. "One second."

The first bouncer turned to him in question, and something flashed in number two's eyes that made him back down.

"What's the problem?" Delaney asked with annoyance.

Number two pinned her with a stare. "Wait," he commanded.

There was an edge to his tone that had her snapping her mouth closed, but his gaze was locked on me. And that singular focus made me shiver.

What the hell had Delaney gotten us into?

CHAPTER THIRTY

Cillian

HE MUSIC BARELY PENETRATED MY OFFICE, EVEN WITH my shifter hearing. It had taken four times the soundproofing humans typically required, but the added time and expense had been worth it. It meant that I could have a sanctuary in the middle of debauchery and chaos.

Maddox reclined on my black leather couch, his back to the one-way windows that gave me a view of the mayhem below. He never cared to see what happened, but I always wanted to see it all. Needed to. Just like I needed countless cameras at both home and work to make sure I had eyes everywhere.

Maddox tapped something on his iPad. "We have a new caster seeking sanctuary."

I leaned back in my chair. "Story?"

He scanned the screen, taking in the details. "Comes from a clan who tends toward dark magic. Didn't want to go that route, so he left. Tried to make it in no-man's-land but got roughed up. Is hoping that living on horde territory will keep him protected."

My fingers tapped along my glass desk. I'd started my dragon horde by accident more than anything. Finding my bond mates had meant the need to mark our own territory, but the life I'd led meant I'd also acquired a rag-tag group of friends. A mixture of all different types of supernaturals, not just dragon shifters. They'd all needed a safe place to call home. And I wasn't about to turn them away.

Word had spread about a safe haven of sorts for supernaturals. So, every so often, we got a request for sanctuary. We didn't always say yes, but most of the time we did.

"Does his story check out?" I asked.

Maddox sent me a droll look. "Do you think I'd be bringing him to you if it hadn't?"

I fought the urge to roll my eyes. "Set a meeting. It wouldn't hurt to have a caster to call on." Their magic could come in handy, especially if someone needed healing.

"Done," Maddox said, typing away. "We need to talk about the Corbett clan."

Just the sound of their name had my back teeth grinding. The only person I hated more than them was my father. And I'd wiped him from the earth just a few weeks ago.

"What. About. Them?" I gritted out.

Maddox's gaze lifted, studying me carefully.

"Don't try to shrink me," I snarled.

Just because the man was teaching now, didn't mean that his psychology degree lay dormant.

"I can't turn my knowledge on and off, Cill," he muttered.

I worked my jaw back and forth, trying to loosen the tension there. It didn't work.

The Corbetts had been a thorn in my side since I'd begun fighting underground in the hopes of simply feeding myself. The alpha, Dexter, had seen my potential and tried to get me to join their horde.

But I'd seen the way he ruled with an iron fist. I knew that kind of leadership, had seen the kind of darkness it could lead to, and hadn't wanted a thing to do with it.

Dexter hadn't been pleased.

He'd pitted his top fighters against me in the ring, trying everything he could to get me to submit. It hadn't worked. When I'd started my own horde, he'd attacked our boundaries time and time again.

When that, too, had failed, we'd come to a tenuous sort of truce. But I knew he was just biding his time. And his son, Hal, was just as hungry for payback.

"What happened?" I growled.

"They're testing our boundaries again. Doing flybys at night. Scoping out our property with long-range cameras during the day."

Fury burned hot and bright. While the club was on neutral ground, the campus and town, including our home, were Teaghlach Clan territory. Gaelic for family. Because that was what we were. Family by choice, which in many cases was stronger than blood.

"This requires retribution." I tried to keep my voice calm, but the anger burning deep made my voice vibrate.

Maddox's face was a careful mask. "What did you have in mind?"

I drummed my fingers on the desk. "Have you figured out a pattern to the flybys?"

He stayed quiet, and I had my answer. Maddox's mind was unlike anything I'd ever experienced before. Genius wasn't even the right term. It was more. Because there was an intuition on top of the intelligence.

"I want two of our enforcers waiting. Tell them to maim, not kill. But if they return, death is the only answer."

A muscle along Maddox's cheek fluttered, but he typed something into the iPad, and I knew he'd sent the order.

"What else?" I asked, eager to move on from the Corbetts. Discussing them unsettled my beast. As it was, I'd need to fly for hours tonight to burn off the anger.

"We need to discuss Knox—"

Maddox's voice was cut off by the ring of my desk phone.

I pushed the button for speakerphone. "McCarthy."

"Hey, boss."

I could hear voices behind Samson and knew he was at his usual post. "What do you need?"

"We might have a problem."

I instantly straightened, on alert. "Talk."

"Your girl's here. Hayden."

My skin rippled, my scales trying to break free at just the sound of her name.

Samson pushed on. "Came with a girl Cal has a deal with. She tips big, and he always lets her and her friends in. What do you want me to do?"

Maddox leaned forward on the couch. He was gripping the iPad so tightly that his knuckles bleached white.

I was quiet for a moment, playing the angles. But it was my beast who won. "Let her in."

I flipped over my phone, wondering why the hell her guards hadn't warned me of her whereabouts. But as I did, I saw a flurry of texts from them with various locations. I'd forgotten I'd put the damned thing on silent.

"Will do, boss."

I hung up and met Maddox's glare.

"What the hell are you playing at, Cill?"

I grinned at him, but there was a feral edge. "Our Little Flame wants to play. Who are we to stop her?"

CHAPTER THIRTY-ONE

Hayden

AS THE BOUNCER OPENED THE DOOR, A WAVE OF HEAT and music hit me. The song had a heavy bass, and the heat was almost oppressive. But still, I followed Maggie and Bella inside.

As soon as the club's interior came into view, I stopped dead. In a million years, I never would've guessed that this was what lay behind industrial walls. Everything read decadent, opulent debauchery.

Black leather booths lined the walls. Each one was crowded with people drinking champagne or harder things. The dance floor was packed with people. Some moving so closely, I wondered if they were doing more than dancing. Above the dance floor were gold metal cages with scantily clad dancers moving to their own rhythm.

My gaze pulled to a massive but still-crowded bar that was absolutely gorgeous. The gleaming dark wood countertop was littered with drinks as bartenders hurried to serve more.

Delaney pushed me farther inside. "Come on, I need a drink."

I swallowed hard and stepped deeper inside the club. I'd been right about the energy; it pulsed all around us, a living, breathing thing.

"Supposedly, there's a secret VIP floor. I've been trying to get us in there, but so far, no luck," Delaney said as she navigated the crowd.

I couldn't imagine what a VIP floor would look like if this was the regular one.

We came to a stop in a crowd waiting for drinks, and Maggie practically bounced on her stilettos. "Isn't this place incredible?" she squealed.

"It's something," I mumbled. And while it certainly wasn't my usual scene, there was *something* about it. The heady feel of so many people searching for fun, for pleasure.

Bella grinned. "It's still early. Things only get crazier."

That had my stomach hollowing. I wasn't sure I could handle crazier.

Delaney laughed, reading the panic on my face. "Relax and live a little, Hayden. It's time to have some fun."

Annoyance fluttered deep inside me as we worked our way toward the bar. I had fun, didn't I? I tried to remember the last thing I'd done that would classify as such.

I thought it was fun studying with Cáel. We snuck in snacks and laughed at the students sneaking off to hook up in the stacks. But somehow, I didn't think Delaney would agree.

She, Maggie, and Bella pushed forward, shouting their orders to the bartender. I gulped when it was my turn. The guy was older than us, probably about twenty-five, and definitely good-looking.

He shot me a wide smile. "What can I get for you, beautiful?"

I leaned forward as the other girls had. "Can you give me something nonalcoholic but make it look like alcohol?"

I let my eyes do the pleading as I leaned back.

He just winked at me. "I've got just the thing."

He set to work making our drinks as the girls chatted. In a

matter of seconds, he was handing them to all of us. When he got to me, he extended his arm with a flourish. "My specialty."

It was in a rocks glass and looked fizzy. When I took a sip, all I tasted was sparkling water and pineapple. I smiled at him appreciatively. "Thank you. It's delicious."

I expected another wink or a grin, but instead, his face paled as he took a massive step back.

Heat flared at my back as someone boxed me in. Lips skimmed the outside of my ear. "I don't think you're old enough to drink, Little Flame."

A pleasant shiver skated over my skin as I whirled around.

Cillian's large frame all but engulfed me. Even though there were a million different scents swirling around us, I could somehow still pick his out of the crowd. It was a smoky cedar and something else I couldn't pin down.

I let my lips close around the straw and took another sip.

Cillian's dark green eyes flashed brighter, and then the color swirled. "Little Flame…"

"It's not alcohol," I admitted.

He chuckled, low and throaty. "Good. Then maybe I won't have to fire my bartender. But based on the way he was looking at you, I probably should."

My stomach dipped and rolled. *What the hell did that mean?*

"What are you doing here?" I asked.

Cillian's mouth curved as though he were trying to smile but didn't quite remember how. "This is my club."

My jaw went slack. "You own Ashes & Emeralds?"

His eyes twinkled in the moving lights. "Yes. Welcome to the lion's den."

Lion's den was absolutely right. My gaze moved over the space, taking it in with new eyes. "How long have you owned it?"

Cillian shrugged, the action making his black button-down pull taut over his broad chest. "About five years now."

"Wow," I mumbled. My gaze moved to his face. "How old are you?"

Those beautiful lips twitched. "Thirty-two. How old are you?"

Something told me he already knew. "Nineteen."

"Start kindergarten late?"

Cillian was still close. So near I could feel the heat coming off his body in waves. It was a kind of proximity that made it hard to answer these kinds of questions honestly.

I shook my head. "Had to repeat a year after my parents died."

The truth was that my nightmares had been so bad I'd been institutionalized for a couple of months.

Cillian's jaw went rock hard. "I'm sorry, Little Flame."

I shrugged, unsure of what else to say.

His hand moved then, coming to my waist and resting there. The heat flared again, pulsing between us. "Why did you come here tonight?"

There was such genuine curiosity in his voice that I found myself answering. "I wanted to know what it's like to be a normal girl."

Those green eyes swirled again, and his hand dropped from my waist. But instead of pulling away, Cillian took my hand and pulled me close. "You want normal?"

My mouth went dry, but I nodded.

"Dance with me."

CHAPTER THIRTY-TWO

Hayden

THE HEAT FROM CILLIAN'S PALM PULSED AGAINST MY skin. It was as if it were a living, breathing thing. This phantom energy that swirled between us.

His dark green eyes flashed with heat, with challenge, with *promise*. "Come on, Little Flame, scared I'll bite?"

Yes. I was scared he'd do more than bite. And I was scared I'd get addicted. But I found myself nodding anyway.

There was a flash of white teeth against the pulsing lights of the club, and I had the sneaking suspicion I'd just made a deal with the devil.

Cillian tugged me away from the bar, and I hurried to set my drink on the counter. He didn't struggle to make his way through the crowd. People parted for him. Maybe it was his size, maybe it was the cold calculation that always seemed to live on his face, but everyone simply moved out of his way.

He came to a stop in the middle of the dance floor. The song changed to a more sultry tune. It still had a heavy bass, but it was slower paced. He pulled me into him, his hard, muscular body pressed against my softer one.

My heart raced as I looked up into those dark green eyes. "I kissed Knox."

There was the faintest twitch of Cillian's lips. Or maybe I just imagined it.

"I know." Cillian swayed our bodies to the beat as if he'd been dancing all his life.

My eyes widened. "You…know…"

He nodded slightly. "I know."

"I didn't take Knox for a bragger," I muttered. But maybe it was for the best. Everything was out in the open, despite the fact that I was feeling a pull toward all the men who lived in that house. Maybe I had a sex addiction I didn't know about.

"He's not," Cillian said. "But we needed to know."

My brow furrowed. "Why?"

Cillian's fingers teased the bare skin of my back, sliding beneath the shirt to my waist. Each swipe of his callused thumb sent a cascade of sparks across my skin.

"We're different, Little Flame."

My breaths came quicker, and I was struggling to keep hold of each inhale.

"Different?" It was the only word I could seem to get out with my body going haywire under Cillian's touch.

He leaned closer, curving his body around mine so I was engulfed. His head dropped to my ear. "What do you think it would be like to have five men devoted to your every need?"

Cillian's fingers skimmed along my waist, tracing some sort of intricate design. My core tightened, and each exhale left me in a sort of pant.

"Every want?" he pushed, his lips skimming my ear.

My mind swam with possibilities and images. Every part of my body flushed hot as I tried to get my brain to function properly. "Easton and Maddox don't even like me."

Cillian chuckled darkly, the vibrations sweeping through me. "Oh, they like you, Little Flame. They just don't want to let themselves."

My breaths came faster, in quick pants.

"Don't get me wrong," he said, his thigh sliding between my legs, the friction almost making me cry out. "They have their reasons. But they won't be able to resist for long."

Cillian's thigh shifted as he moved our bodies to the beat. I couldn't help the soft mewl that escaped my lips.

He growled in my ear in response. "So sensitive."

I bit the inside of my cheek, trying to get my body under control. "Does Knox know?"

Cillian pulled back a fraction, his eyes hooded. "Does he know that I'm going to take you to bed sometime soon and fuck you so hard you'll feel me for days? Yes, Little Flame, he does. And he likes it."

My lips parted on a gasp. It was the kind of statement that should've deserved a slap, but instead, I felt wetness gather between my thighs.

Cillian's hand lifted to my face, his thumb tracing my bottom lip. "You like that idea."

"I-I don't know."

His lips did twitch now. "Your body likes it. I can smell you, Little Flame. And I can't wait to shove my face between those pretty thighs and eat you until you scream."

My core spasmed as my mind filled with that image.

"Cillian," I breathed.

A hand tapped on Cillian's shoulder, and he whirled, a snarl on his face. "What?"

The man paled but moved in closer to whisper in his ear.

The expression on Cillian's face went even more thunderous, but he jerked his head in a nod and then turned back to me. His hands came to my face, tender this time. "I have to go."

My mind whirled. He was going to drop these bombs, turn my body up to eleven, and then just *leave*?

Cillian seemed to read my thoughts. "I'm sorry. I'd stay if I could. I'd drag you into that back hall and make you come on my fingers."

Another spasm, low and vicious.

"Soon, Little Flame. Soon."

And then he was gone.

I stood in the middle of the dance floor, unmoving. I wasn't sure just how long I stayed there. A couple knocked into me, finally jerking me out of my stupor. I had no idea where the girls I'd come here with were. Hell, they'd probably already ditched.

I wove my way through the crowd. They didn't part for me the way they had for Cillian. I was jostled and bumped but finally made it to the outskirts of the dance floor. The moment I did, a hand closed around my arm and tugged me hard.

I readied my defensive strike but relaxed the moment I saw it was Delaney.

She was anything *but* relaxed. "How the hell do you know Cillian McCarthy?"

I fought the groan that wanted to surface. "He's friends with Knox."

"I know that. But how do *you* know him? No one gets close to him. The only time he comes out of that office in the sky is when a high roller comes in or if he needs to personally kick someone's ass."

Her gaze had flicked to the windows up above as she spoke, and I followed her line of sight. You couldn't see through them, but I'd bet anything he could see out. Was he watching now? Had he seen me enter and come down to find me? My skin prickled, but it wasn't a bad sensation. It was as if my body were aware of *everything*.

"Hayden," Delaney snapped.

My focus came back to her. "Sorry, what?"

Redness crept up her throat. "How. Do. You. Know. Him?" she gritted out.

"I went to dinner at their house, remember?"

That redness only grew. "One dinner and he's pulling you onto the dance floor?"

Maggie and Bella appeared behind her, both looking a little tipsy.

Maggie fanned herself. "It was hooooot."

Delaney whirled on her. "Shut up."

Oh, jeez. This wasn't good. Was it Knox that Delaney wanted or all of them? Not that I could throw stones. I'd kissed one, practically come with another, and spent every night with a third. God, did that make me an awful human? Maybe it did.

Delaney turned back to me, her gorgeous, dark hair swishing around her as she did. "Just watch out," she huffed. "I've heard if people cross Cillian McCarthy, they tend to disappear."

Chapter Thirty-Three

Cillian

MY BLOOD WAS FIRE, AND I'D PROBABLY MADE POOR Greg shit himself at the force of my fury. Typically, I had better control than this. But normally, I wasn't surrounded by the sweet smell of my mate, by her need.

My beast pushed against my skin, wanting out, wanting free. He didn't understand why we hadn't already claimed Hayden. He wanted me to bite her right there on the dance floor and then drag her home to fuck her long and hard.

Who was I kidding? I wanted the same damn thing. But I also didn't want to terrify her.

Hayden had no idea that she was a dragon. No idea what it meant to be mated. This wasn't a casual dating situation. This was our souls being bound for all eternity.

I stormed up the stairs to the second level. The guards at the entry to the floor wisely took a step back when they saw me coming.

That internal fire was brewing, needing to be set free. I needed that flight, that or hit the heavy bag on repeat.

I stalked down the hallway to my office, ripping the door open.

Cáel turned at my entrance, curiosity and maybe a hint of amusement on his face. When was the last time I'd seen a hint of humor in his expression? Probably when he'd disemboweled a Corbett who had tried to sneak into our territory.

But Maddox? He was furious. The most stoic and serious of our bond, he rarely let his emotions show. He was too calm and collected for that.

But now? He was letting it all out.

Maddox prowled toward me, reminding me of the lethal creature that lay beneath the surface. "What were you thinking?"

My brows lifted at that. "Excuse me?"

Maddox gave me a hard shove. "You all but flayed Knox's ass for kissing her, and you're on the dance floor, two seconds away from fucking her?"

My back teeth ground together. He had a point. But I hadn't crossed the line. I hadn't kissed Hayden. I hadn't made her come. But if Greg hadn't interrupted when he had, I probably would've. "It was under control."

Cáel let out a grunt that I knew was his version of a laugh.

"That was playing with fire," Maddox accused. "She doesn't know what she's getting into. It isn't fair."

Fire was exactly the right word. My Little Flame had burned me in a way that would leave permanent scars. And I loved every second of it.

"Whether she knows it or not, the truth remains the same," I growled. Hayden was ours. She was a dragon. It didn't matter that she was unaware. She felt the same pull that we all did.

It killed me that it confused her. I could see the guilt playing across her face as her body responded to mine. She felt like she was betraying Knox, even though there'd been no promises made there.

Hayden's heart was all goodness, loyalty, and kindness. She was exactly the kind of mate I'd dreamed of but never thought I would find.

"We need to tell her. Soon. This is too hard on her."

Maddox's eyes flashed gold. "Too hard on her or too hard on you?"

I shoved him back, sending him falling onto the leather couch. "You didn't see her. She's feeling incredibly guilty for being pulled toward all of us. It's tearing her up inside."

Cáel stiffened at that. "She's hurting?"

I glanced at him. "Yes. She's all goodness and light. She doesn't understand that what she's feeling is perfectly normal."

"We need to tell her. Now," Cáel demanded.

He wouldn't be able to handle Hayden in any sort of pain, physical or emotional. He'd do whatever it took to stop it.

"Both of you need to get a grip. What do you think is going to happen when we tell her? She's going to freak and run to the cops," Maddox snarled.

Cáel shook his head roughly. "She wouldn't."

Maddox glared at him. "You've known her for two-point-five seconds. You have no idea what she'll do. We need time to get her to trust us. Then we tell her."

Cáel bared his teeth at Maddox. "I *know* Hayden. She's my mate. She trusts me."

Maddox let out a huff as if to say, *idiot.*

"Once one of us shifts for her, she'll believe. And once Easton has skin-to-skin contact with her, her own path to trans-formation will begin," I said, trying to bring some control back to my voice.

When a dragon shifter was traumatized at a young age, it could take the presence of his or her bond to bring out their dragon. Sometimes, there was too much damage for the dragon to emerge, but I knew Hayden was stronger than that. Her dragon, too.

Maddox's jaw worked back and forth. "And are you going to force Easton to do that, Alpha?"

A growl gathered in my throat. "You know I'm not that kind

of leader." I'd never force a member of my horde to do something that went against their wishes.

"Well, he's not going to do it of his own free will," Maddox snapped.

I wasn't so sure. As much as Easton wanted to keep his distance from Hayden, I saw those walls starting to crumble. He wasn't immune to her effect.

"We need to give her the choice," Cáel said quietly. "And that means telling her everything. I don't feel right about hiding all of this from her."

My gut churned at that. He was right. The longer the secrets remained, the more betrayed Hayden would feel when we finally told her. We needed to find a way to tell her the truth, soon.

"You're both idiots," Maddox grumbled.

But I wondered just how much of this was Maddox's fear of exposure and how much of it was his fear of breaking. Once Hayden knew the truth, he'd have one less wall between them. It would only be his position with the university holding him back from her. And I didn't think Maddox was ready to let himself fall.

My phone buzzed in my back pocket, and I pulled it out. The name *James* flashed across the screen, and a lead weight settled in my gut. I tapped the screen. "What?"

"We have a problem, Alpha."

"Tell me," I clipped.

"There are about a dozen Corbetts in the club. I just spotted three. Sean's clocking more."

Gaelic curses spewed from my mouth. "Secure Hayden, now. Bring her to my office."

If the Corbetts scented her, there would be war for sure. And how the hell had they made it onto the premises? While the club was neutral territory, they were not welcome, and my bouncers would've never let them in.

"Understood—"

James's words cut off. There was a grunt and a gurgle and then nothing at all.

"James," I barked.

Nothing.

"James," I yelled again.

Then a sound came over the line. A dark chuckle. "I'm sorry. James can't come to the phone right now."

And my blood turned to ice.

CHAPTER THIRTY-FOUR

Hayden

I TRIED TO REMEMBER MY VOW OF ATTEMPTING A NIGHT OF normality, but it was basically useless. Delaney's words kept echoing in my ears. *"I've heard if people cross Cillian McCarthy, they tend to disappear."*

That meant drug dealer, right? It had to. That, or some gang.

The contents of my stomach churned and rolled. What did it say about me that, as worried as I was, I couldn't get myself to decide to walk away? Whatever they were mixed up in, it couldn't be good.

"Earth to Hayden," Maggie singsonged, tipping over against Bella.

I shook myself out of my spiraling thoughts. "Sorry. What'd you say?"

She grinned. "I asked if you got a feel for Cillian's dick. I heard it's a monster."

My cheeks heated at the insinuation.

Bella let out a strangled laugh. "Jesus, Maggie. Get ahold of yourself. You're ready to throw Hayden to the wolves just to get some info about Cillian's cock?"

Maggie shrugged. "Sacrifices must be made. I'd sacrifice my-self for—"

"Shut up," Delaney snapped.

I bit the inside of my cheek as I studied her. Her pissed-off state hadn't lessened, but she was the only one who seemed to have details I desperately needed about the guys. So, I took a deep breath and asked, "What do you know about him?"

Delaney's annoyed gaze turned to me, and it was as if she were trying to decide whether to tell me.

"It seems like you know them pretty well," I added quickly, hoping that a stroke to her ego would be the ticket.

I was right. Delaney couldn't help herself if it would let her circle know she was *so* much more in the know than the rest of us. She straightened her shoulders. "Cillian runs Ember Hollow."

I frowned. "He's the mayor or something?"

Delaney laughed. "Hardly. He runs things behind the scenes. I've heard that he started making money when he was fighting in the underground circuit."

My stomach pitched. I knew she was right about that. Cillian had told me as much.

"He had a big fight when he was twenty. It was against this fighter everyone thought he would lose to. Cillian borrowed money from a loan shark and put every penny he had on himself. The odds were twenty to one or something crazy like that," Delaney continued.

"He won," I said quietly.

She grinned. "Yep. Became a millionaire overnight."

Because Cillian had believed in himself. Pride surged through me for him.

"He just kept taking gambles. This club. Several other businesses. The stock market. He's a billionaire now," Delaney continued.

"Billionaire with a B?" I squeaked.

"Yep. And famously private. He doesn't let people onto his

property. Doesn't let them get close. Doesn't trust anyone but that so-called family he's created. So, it makes me curious why he's getting so close to you."

A chill skittered down my spine. "I honestly don't know. I think it's just because Knox and I are friends."

Delaney scoffed. "Sure."

I swallowed hard. "I'm going to find a bathroom. I'll be back."

I hurried away from the group before any of them could argue. I wound my way through the crowd in search of a restroom. The first hallway I found was packed with people, and the lines to the bathrooms were ridiculously long.

So, I kept going, finding my way to the back of the club. There was another hallway tucked behind the raised dais the DJ was on. This one was surprisingly quiet and people-free. Two signs illuminated restrooms.

I hurried toward the one for ladies and slipped inside. I didn't actually have to pee. I needed to breathe.

Crossing to the sinks, I ran the water as cold as it would go. I held my hands beneath the stream, hoping it would cool me down. But I could still feel Cillian's fingers trailing over my back and around my waist.

"Stop it," I snapped.

I had to get myself under control. I'd never been the kind of girl who fell prey to her hormones. I made smart choices. I didn't fall for pretty smiles and hushed promises because I knew they could end up being beyond empty.

Shutting off the water, I reached for some paper towels. I took my time drying my hands. No more stupid-girl moves. I would keep my distance from the guys. I'd focus on my studies and my job. Knox and Cáel and I could be friends but nothing more. And I was steering clear of Cillian altogether.

I felt better with that decision made, more in control. Tossing the paper towels into the trash, I stepped back into the hallway and blinked. Was it darker? That was weird.

I took two steps toward the club before strong arms jerked me back against a broad chest.

"What do we have here?" a voice sneered in my ear, the rank breath filling my nose.

I struggled to get free, sending an elbow backward as I'd learned in my self-defense classes. But the man just chuckled.

"Nice try, bitch." He grabbed my hair, pulling it so hard my eyes filled with tears. "I heard the Teaghlach clan had a new whore. Didn't think I'd get you on the first try. They're getting sloppy."

I writhed and struggled, letting out a scream. But the sounds were swallowed by the club's music.

The man just laughed as two more stepped out of the shadows. "What do you say, boys? Should we have a little taste before we rip her to shreds?"

Everything in me turned to ice. This wasn't happening. It couldn't.

The man leaned in, licking the side of my neck. Then he stilled, gripping me tighter. "What the hell?" he snarled. "Dragon?" he breathed, almost reverently.

I squirmed and kicked, trying to get free.

"No, you don't," he growled. "You're coming with us."

He dragged me toward the door, and my panic flared hot and bright. I couldn't let him get me out of there. Couldn't let them get me to a secondary location.

His arm looped around my neck as he dragged me, and I bit down as hard as I could on his forearm.

The man howled in pain, his hold on me loosening a fraction. I didn't wait. I ran. But the two other men were waiting.

"I don't think so, bitch," the taller one snarled.

But his words were cut off as a blade sliced across his throat from behind.

And I did the only thing I could. I screamed.

CHAPTER THIRTY-FIVE

Hayden

THE MAN CRUMPLED TO THE FLOOR IN FRONT OF ME, revealing Cáel, fury streaking across his face. I didn't know whether to run toward him or away. But I didn't have a chance to make up my mind.

The second man lunged for me, knocking me into a wall so hard I saw stars. I struggled against his hold as Cáel shouted something. The man's fist connected with my face, and my vision went blurry.

Everything was so hazy that I couldn't see who had ripped me from my attacker's arms. I writhed and fought with what little strength I had. "Easy, Little One. It's me."

The scent of snow and campfire filled my nose, and I slumped against Cáel.

"I've got you. Just hold on."

Sounds of fighting filled the hallway. My vision slowly cleared just as Cillian punched out with some unseen blade. The man who'd punched me gurgled, blood spilling from his mouth as he crumpled to the floor.

Cillian wiped his hand on the man's shirt and then spat on him, uttering something in a foreign language.

Maddox shouted something as he fought with my first attacker, and Cillian joined him in the fray. Within a matter of seconds, that man was on the floor, bleeding out, too.

Cillian turned to us before that man had even taken his last breath. "We need to move. They'll have called for reinforcements."

Cáel jerked his head in a nod, striding toward the back door. "Close your eyes, Little One. You don't need to see them."

But I couldn't make myself. Three bodies. So much blood.

Images of my mother's fallen form filled my head. I shook violently against Cáel, and he cursed.

Then we were outside, the cold air wrapping around us. Cáel jogged toward a blacked-out SUV as Cillian beeped the locks, and we were inside.

Cáel held me as Maddox's hands moved gently over my face.

"Where does it hurt, *Mo Ghràidh*?" Concern and maybe pain twisted his features.

My teeth chattered violently, and I couldn't get any words out.

"He hit her," Cáel growled.

I could feel the fury coming off him in waves. Felt the ragged, quick breaths beneath me. I knew that he was seconds away from losing it.

I couldn't speak, but I nuzzled into Cáel's neck, trying to reassure him I was all right.

A rumbling sound that was a lot like a roar emanated from Cáel's chest.

Maddox's eyes flashed to him. "Hold it together. We need to get her to safety."

The tires of the SUV squealed as if to punctuate the point.

"We've got backup in the air and on the ground," Cillian clipped. "But I want to know how the hell they got in."

"Traitor," Cáel gritted out.

Cillian's fingers tightened on the wheel. "They'll die for this. Slowly."

My body shook harder.

"Enough," Maddox barked. "You're scaring her."

His hands were on my face again. "I need to examine you, okay, Hayden?"

I nodded slowly.

Maddox pulled something from the back seat, wincing as he did so. I couldn't see what was in the black leather bag, but a second later, a small light was flashing across my eyes.

I squinted against it, recoiling.

"I'm sorry, *Mo Ghràidh*," he whispered. "I need to see if you have a concussion."

I swallowed. "It's...okay." My words were shaky at best, but at least I'd gotten them out.

The light moved across my eyes again, and the brightness hurt.

"Headache?" he asked.

"Yes," I admitted.

"Nausea?" he inquired as he pulled the light back.

"Maybe—" My words cut off as that beam illuminated Maddox's shirt.

Cold panic ripped through me. "Maddox!" I jerked upright, not caring that my head swam with the action. "You've been cut."

I was already tugging at his shirt as Cillian cursed and increased his speed.

"How bad?" Cillian clipped.

"It's just a nick," Maddox said, trying to capture my hands. "I'm all right."

"No, you're not," I growled as I took in the wound. "We need to get you to the hospital. This is really deep."

"I can treat it at home," he argued.

"Are you a doctor or something?" I snapped.

He grinned at me, the first time I'd seen him truly smile, and it was devastating. "Medic, actually. I have EMT training."

"Oh," I muttered, then pawed through the medical bag. "I still doubt you'll be able to stitch yourself up."

He grunted. "Done it before."

I stilled at that. Was this sort of thing normal for them? I couldn't think about that now.

I pulled out a bottle of peroxide and a trauma pad, then looked up at Maddox. "I'm sorry. This might hurt."

Maddox just jerked his chin in a nod. "Do it."

I poured the peroxide on his wound, and Maddox didn't make a sound. Then I pressed the gauze pad to his injury.

Maddox sucked in a breath as our eyes locked.

"I'm so sorry." Tears filled my eyes.

His hand lifted to cup my cheek. "No tears, *Mo Ghràidh*. They slay me."

"He hurt you because of me. Because you were trying to protect me."

Maddox's thumb stroked my face. "I'd take a blade for you a thousand times."

My eyes burned as my head swam. "Why?"

"Because you matter."

It was so simple, but it shredded everything inside of me. I tried to swallow down the emotions, to keep them at bay, but I couldn't. I felt the hot tears track down my cheeks. "What's happening?" I whispered.

Pain streaked across Maddox's face. "We'll explain. I promise. We just—we need to deal with a few things first."

A low growl sounded from the front of the SUV, which made the whole vehicle shake.

My body began to tremble, and Cáel held me tighter. "It's okay, Little One. We'll keep you safe."

But I wasn't sure he was right. Something told me that walking into these guys' lives had put me in more danger than ever.

CHAPTER THIRTY-SIX

Hayden

"I'VE GOT IT," MADDOX SAID, TAKING THE GAUZE PAD FROM my hold and keeping pressure on it.

I moved to lean back against Cáel, and a wave of dizziness swept over me.

"Little One," Cáel growled. "What's wrong?"

"Oh, I don't know, random attacks and multiple dead bodies."

Cáel just grunted as the SUV turned onto the gravel road. Each jostle of the vehicle reminded me of the beating my body had taken. My head and face throbbed, and my neck ached. I wanted to find a bathtub and submerge myself in it for a year.

Cáel tucked me into him, and I inhaled his snowy, campfire scent. Everything about it calmed me. As though my body knew that if I was in his hold, I would always be completely safe.

Cillian slowed at the gate to their property, and several men dressed in black stepped out of the shadows.

My entire body locked.

"Shhhh," Cáel whispered. "It's just security."

I relaxed a fraction. "Why do you need this kind of security?"

Cáel and Maddox shared a look, and dread swamped me. What the hell had I gotten myself caught up in?

The moment the guards registered who was behind the wheel, the gates began to open. Cillian didn't say a word as he guided the SUV toward the house. In a matter of minutes, he was pulling to a stop.

Two figures were through the door in an instant.

I braced but relaxed when I saw it was Knox and Easton.

Cáel opened our door and stepped out, with me still in his arms.

"Hayden!" Knox yelled, striding toward us.

"Let me down," I whispered. Cáel's holding me would just make Knox more worried.

He grunted but obeyed.

The moment my feet touched the ground, I knew I'd made a mistake. My legs wobbled, and the world around me swam.

Knox cursed as I wavered on my feet. But it was too late. I was already falling.

⌒

"How the hell did you let this happen?" Easton snarled at someone I couldn't see.

Couldn't see because I was floating on a cloud. Some part of me felt pain pulsing in my head; another part recognized that I had to be with the guys. But I couldn't see them. Couldn't see anything but swirling blackness all around.

"Watch. Your. Tone," Cillian gritted out. "We didn't *let* anything happen. And trust me when I say we will find the traitor, and he will pay."

Cáel let out a low growl of agreement. "I want in on that retribution."

"Are you sure we shouldn't take her to the hospital?" Knox asked.

His voice was closer than the rest, and I felt it then. His hand in mine, his thumb tracing designs on my skin. Heat pulsed there, comfort.

I wanted to open my eyes but couldn't quite get there.

"No," Maddox clipped. "The healer examined her. We can't risk them finding something in her bloodwork."

I felt myself frown. *Healer? Bloodwork?*

"You all should've been watching her better," Easton snarled. "And what about her guards?"

Guards? What was he talking about?

Cillian let out a growl. "James tried to protect her, and he paid with his life. Sean is touch and go."

Easton muttered a curse. "I'm sorry—I just—what the hell is happening?"

"We have to assume the Corbetts know about Hayden now. They'll do everything they can to take her," Cillian said, voice low.

Cáel let out a noise that sounded more animal than human. "That's not going to happen."

"No," Cillian agreed. "It's not. But we're going to have to tighten security in every way. We need to move Hayden into the house."

"No," Easton clipped.

There were sounds of a scuffle.

"You'd seriously put your bullshit fears above our mate's safety?" Cillian demanded.

"It's not bullshit," Easton shot back. "And you know it."

"Enough," Maddox said, his voice full of exhaustion. "This is where she has to be. We'll deal with it, Easton. She's more important."

My mind struggled to pull together the pieces of their conversation, but none of them made sense, and my brain was foggy at best. I let out a sound of frustration.

Knox's hand spasmed around mine. "I think she's waking up." He squeezed my hand, purposefully this time. "Hayden?"

I wanted to open my eyes. I didn't want to be stuck in this weird alternate universe anymore. But my eyelids felt so heavy.

A palm ghosted over my hair. "Come on, Little Flame. Show us those violet eyes."

A prickle of awareness came with Cillian's touch, one more thing pulling me back to the present. My eyelids fluttered against the low light of the room. It was a sea of blue. Everything about it was peaceful and serene.

"There she is," Cillian said softly, his voice rough.

"How do you feel?" Knox asked, his thumb still sweeping across my skin.

Five sets of eyes waited expectantly for an answer. I took a mental inventory. I felt like I'd been caught in a riptide and banged against a few rocks.

"Okay," I croaked but winced at the single word.

"Liar," Cillian accused.

I grimaced. "Head and face hurt."

"I'll get an ice pack," Cáel said, quickly leaving the room, a murderous expression on his face.

"Where are the fucking pain meds?" Easton snapped.

Maddox shook his head. "She needs to eat a little something first. If she takes them on an empty stomach, she'll just be sick."

A muscle fluttered in Easton's cheek. "Then get her something to goddamned eat."

My brows pulled together, the action making the pain in my face flare.

Easton seemed to register the discomfort because he grabbed some sort of ceramic object and hurled it at the wall.

Maddox was in his face in a flash. "Pull it together. Now. This is the last thing Hayden needs."

Easton snapped his rage-filled eyes in my direction. There

was so much fury there, as if it were my fault that I'd been attacked. His jaw hardened to granite, and he stalked out of the room.

I watched him go, trying to understand his reaction. "I thought he didn't even like me."

Knox released his hold on my hand and pushed to his feet, sorrow filling his expression. "He likes you too much. That's the problem."

Chapter Thirty-Seven

Cáel

THE RAGE SWIRLING INSIDE ME FED MY BEAST. HE pushed against my skin, demanding freedom, demanding to hunt the ones who had hurt our mate. I tried everything I could to calm him, telling him that they were dead and that Hayden was safe. But none of it was of any use.

Because we both knew that while the immediate threat was over, a far greater one loomed.

My jaw cracked as I tried to loosen it, but the tension wouldn't leave. I gathered an ice pack and a snack that I thought would be easy on Hayden's stomach.

Pain dug its vicious claws into my chest as I pictured her bruised face and confused expression. She had no idea what she'd gotten herself into, what she'd been born into. But I couldn't be sorry that we'd found her. Or maybe it was more accurate to say that she'd found us.

She soothed my beast in a way that I'd never experienced. My brothers had noticed the change, too. I wasn't flying off the handle as much. Not until someone had been a threat to her…

My dragon surged, demanding we get back to Hayden. I didn't fight him on the request because I needed to be back in her presence, too. I needed to assure myself that she was okay, breathing.

A door slammed at the front of the house, and I strode into the foyer just as Knox descended the stairs, a pained expression on his face.

"What happened?" I demanded.

He shook his head. "Easton. He's...not handling this well."

I muttered a curse as I glanced toward the closed front door. We all had our baggage. None of us had come out of our childhoods or young adulthoods unscathed. But East and I...we dealt with it similarly. I got him. But I also wasn't the best at *talking* about it.

"Do you want me to talk to him?" I asked.

Knox swallowed. "No. It's gotta be me."

And I knew what a sacrifice that was for him. Knox liked to see the world as glass half full all the time. For him, that meant ignoring what had happened to his family. He didn't like to go there. The only one he'd likely do it for was Easton.

I reached out and clamped a hand on Knox's shoulder. It was awkward and unpracticed. I wasn't used to touching people. But I wanted Knox to know I had his back. "Just call if you need me."

Knox jerked his head in a nod and moved for the door.

I headed back up the stairs and toward my room to find Maddox sweeping up the remnants of one of my sculptures. My gaze flicked to Cillian in question.

He grimaced. "East."

Shit. He really was on edge. At least he didn't shift in the middle of the house. That'd be one way to let Hayden in on our secret.

Just the thought of her name had my focus pulling to her. She looked so tiny in my massive bed, way paler than normal, too. I crossed toward her, that rage spiking again at the darkening bruise on her face.

I set the ice pack and bottle of apple juice on the nightstand, then untucked the box of crackers from under my arm. "Here," I said quietly. "Let's get this on your face."

As gently as possible, I lifted the ice pack to her cheek.

Hayden's hand covered mine as she took it. "Thank you."

I jerked my head in a nod. "I brought you some crackers and juice."

Maddox dumped the tiny ceramic pieces into a trash can. "Once you eat that, there are pain meds on the nightstand."

"Okay," Hayden agreed, far too easily.

This wasn't how my Little One normally acted. She was full of fire, fighting us every step of the way. Seeing her so easily agreeable, so quiet, felt all sorts of wrong.

A ringtone pierced the air, and Cillian tugged his phone from his pocket. "Talk."

As he listened to the voice on the other end, his expression darkened. "Detain him, and I'll meet you at the shed."

My beast pushed at my skin. He knew what this meant. They'd located a traitor suspect. My dragon wanted vengeance more than his next breath. The only thing he wanted more was the closeness to Hayden.

Maddox pushed to his feet, looking at me. "Do you want to go with Cill or stay here?"

I was torn, but in the end, there was only one answer. "I need to stay."

Surprise flashed in Maddox's amber eyes. He'd never known me to walk away from a chance for bloodshed. "Okay. I'll text with updates."

"Thanks."

Cillian shoved his phone into his pocket and bent to brush his lips across Hayden's temple. "I'll be back, Little Flame. Rest."

She didn't respond at all, and I wondered if shock was settling in.

Cillian's gaze locked with mine. "Keep a close eye."

I grunted in response. He knew I wouldn't let Hayden out of my sight.

The moment the door closed, I toed off my shoes and climbed into bed next to Hayden. She didn't hesitate; she simply curled into me.

Relief swept through me at her seeking comfort in my arms. Some part of me had feared that once she'd seen the monster within, she'd never look at me the same.

My arms curled around her. "I've got you, Little One."

"What's happening?" she whispered.

I couldn't lie, not to Hayden. But I couldn't tell her the full story either. I brushed a hand up and down her spine. "There are people who want to harm us. And they want to harm anyone we care about, too."

Hayden's head tipped back, the ice pack falling away. "You care about me?"

I stared into those violet eyes. "I'd do anything for you."

She swallowed hard. "They were going to hurt me."

A muscle twitched along my jaw. "No one is going to touch you. Never again."

Hayden burrowed deeper into my hold. "I keep feeling him grab me. I can smell his breath."

I struggled to keep my grip on her gentle. "It's going to take time, but the memories will fade. I promise."

That wasn't entirely a lie. But it wasn't completely the truth, either. My demons still haunted me on a regular basis, even if they'd dulled a fraction with time.

"You sound like you have experience with that."

I looked down at my mate. I never talked about my past with anyone, not ever. But I somehow wanted to share a piece of it with her. I swallowed the bile trying to surge up my throat. "I was taken as a child. Tortured."

Hayden gasped, her beautiful lips parting as she sucked in air. Tears filled her eyes. "Cáel."

Her reaction was so instant, so real. It wasn't pity like I'd seen in the past. It was empathy.

A tear slid down her cheek, and I wiped it away. "I'm okay. You help quiet the memories."

Hayden's breaths came faster as she moved just a bit closer. Her mouth was so close I swore I could already taste it.

A war lit inside me. Hayden didn't know the truth yet. And I knew she needed it. But the die had been cast. The fact that Cillian, Mad, and I had all killed for her had cemented our tether.

Still, I should wait.

But I didn't.

I bent, taking her mouth as gently as I could. But the moment her taste filled me, I nearly snapped. The push to claim her was so strong that I almost shifted right then and there.

Hayden let out a little moan as my tongue stroked hers, and my dick stiffened against the zipper of my jeans.

I tore my mouth away from hers, breathing heavily.

Hayden's fingers lifted to her lips. "Oh, shit."

My lips twitched at that, and I kissed her forehead. "Sleep, Little One. Save the freak-out for tomorrow."

CHAPTER THIRTY-EIGHT

Hayden

CONSCIOUSNESS PULLED AT ME. I WAS HOT. TOO HOT. I dreamt that fire licked along my skin, but some part of me knew that it wasn't real.

My eyelids fluttered, revealing darkness around me. It took a moment for my eyes to adjust and to remember where I was. Cáel's room.

It was then that my body became aware of exactly its situation. A large arm was slung over my waist, pulling me against a hard, naked chest. I knew it was Cáel without even looking. It was as if my body recognized his energy or something.

But there was someone else in front of me. I registered his scent before my eyes could make out his face. Pine and rain. Knox.

His deep breaths fluttered the wisps of light brown hair that were falling across his face. He looked so peaceful, so relaxed, so beautiful.

Knox's long lashes fluttered as if his body were attuned to mine, some part of him knowing I was awake. Green eyes took me in. He stared for a long moment. "Are you hurting?"

I took a moment to search my body. "No," I said honestly.

Concern laced his expression. "What woke you up? Nightmare?"

I shook my head slightly. "I was hot."

A grin pulled at Knox's mouth. "You've got a Cáel blanket keeping you warm."

He didn't seem upset by this. Quite the opposite. He seemed...pleased.

Did Knox know that Cáel and I had kissed? That Cillian and I had danced what felt like a lifetime ago? Panic raced through me.

"What's going on in that beautiful brain?" he asked softly.

"It doesn't...bother you?"

Knox's hand lifted to my face. His fingers traced my features in a soothing pattern. "I know it's new to you, but I've always known there would be one woman for me *and* my brothers."

My eyes flared. "You have?"

He nodded, a finger tracing my lips. "It's how we all grew up. It's our...culture."

My mind spun. Were they in some sort of cult or something?

A low chuckle escaped Knox. "I love watching those wheels turn. I know it'll take some getting used to, but be honest. Do you feel drawn to all of us? To Cáel and Cillian and Maddox and Easton?"

I didn't miss the shadow that passed over his eyes as he spoke his brother's name. But I couldn't lie, not to Knox, not when he was being vulnerable with me.

"Yes," I breathed.

Relief washed over him.

"But," I hurried to go on, "not all of those people feel drawn to me, Knox."

He shook his head, his thumb sweeping gently across my bruised cheek. "Mad and East each have their own baggage, but that doesn't mean they don't want you."

I wasn't so sure about that, and my uncertainty must have registered on my face because Knox brushed his lips across mine.

"Just give it time. Let things unfold naturally."

Easy for him to say.

"Why are you having a heart-to-heart in the middle of the night?" Cáel grumbled behind me.

I couldn't help it. I giggled. The expulsion of air and tension felt like heaven after holding so much in.

"It's your fault," Knox shot back. "You're an overgrown heater."

Cáel just pulled me tighter against him, and I didn't miss the hard length that nestled against my ass. My core clenched, heat spreading through me.

"I'm cozy," Cáel retorted.

Knox arched an eyebrow. "Cozy? Since when does the Lord of Pain say *cozy*?"

"Shut up," Cáel growled.

They bantered back and forth, but I couldn't hear a word because my skin felt like it was on fire. Need pulsed between my legs. My breasts felt heavy, and my nipples pebbled.

Knox froze mid-sentence, his nostrils flaring. "Hayden?"

My breaths came quicker.

Cáel muttered a curse. "Are you hurting, Little One?"

I nodded, words escaping me.

His fingers trailed lower, to the hem of my pajama pants that had magically appeared for me last night. "Aching?"

The air caught in my throat. "Yes."

"Want me to ease it?" Cáel whispered hoarsely.

"Please," I begged.

It was all Cáel needed. His hand slid lower, cupping my heat.

I moaned, arching back into him as he slid two fingers inside me.

Knox cursed, his hands going to the buttons on my pajama top. In a matter of seconds, my breasts were free. "God, I knew you'd be beautiful."

He palmed the swells, his thumbs circling my nipples. The touch was almost painful. I needed more. To be filled, stretched. I wanted both of them, now, everywhere.

Knox bent his head, lips closing around one peak and sucking hard.

My mouth opened, silently begging for more.

Cáel slid a third finger inside me. They stroked and teased. As they curled, I cried out. But I needed more.

"Please," I begged.

Cáel's other hand circled my clit, just shy of where I needed him most.

Nonsensical sounds escaped me, pleading for I didn't know what.

Knox's mouth left my breast. "Make her shatter, brother. Tell me what it feels like to have her strangle your fingers like she's going to strangle my cock."

The words had my core convulsing with need.

Cáel cursed just as his fingers found that bundle of nerves.

Knox's lips closed around my nipple again, working it with his tongue. Just as Cáel's fingers stroked inside me, Knox bit down lightly on that peak.

Pleasure and pain rolled through me in a riptide. It held me captive, crashing over me again and again, as Cáel and Knox wrang every ounce of pleasure out of me. Just when I thought I was done, it would start all over again. Until finally, I simply passed out.

Chapter Thirty-Nine

Hayden

I woke alone. Blinking against the morning light, I tried to remember if the memories from last night were a dream or reality. The slight twinge between my legs told me they were very real.

Heat hit my cheeks, and I quickly sat up. The room spun for a moment, but that didn't last long, and my gaze settled on a note perched against the lamp.

Come downstairs when you wake up. Clothes are in the bathroom.

Studying every night with Cáel meant I recognized his hand-writing. But remembering where those hands had been had me blushing all over again.

Part of me wondered if I could just sneak out and call an Uber. But then I remembered the events of early in the night. A cold shiver wracked my body.

Those men. All the blood.

I shoved it down, far away. Having to face my sexcapades would be far better than facing those memories.

Pushing to my feet, I headed for the bathroom. I flicked on the light and took in the space. It was stunning. All white marble and pale blue accents. Like the bedroom, it was serene and peaceful.

I crossed to the sinks and found a pile of clothes in my size, along with a toothbrush and an array of skincare items far fancier than I'd ever used before. As my gaze lifted, I caught sight of my nasty bruise in the mirror. That was going to be fun to explain.

I made quick work of getting ready and pulled on the clothing. The sweater was a lavender cashmere, the same color as my eyes, and the jeans fit me perfectly. When had one of the guys had time to get this stuff?

Shoving that thought from my brain, I headed downstairs.

The faint sounds of conversation pulled me in the direction of the dining room we'd eaten in the night I'd come for dinner. That visit felt like a lifetime ago.

As I moved closer to the dining room, I could just make out Cillian's voice above the rest. "The traitor has been *dealt* with."

I frowned as I rounded the corner, but the moment I stepped inside the room, all conversation stopped, and five sets of eyes came to me. I swallowed hard, knowing my face was likely the shade of a tomato.

Cillian pushed his chair back and stood, crossing to me. He wasn't wearing that black suit anymore, but a white tee that pulled taut across his chest and gray joggers that had my mouth going dry.

Cillian framed my face with his hands. "How are you feeling, Little Flame?"

"Okay," I croaked.

He bent, brushing his lips featherlight across mine. "Good. Sit. Eat."

As Cillian pulled back, I caught sight of Easton glowering at us.

"Don't," Cáel warned lowly, his gaze locked on Easton.

Easton opened his mouth and then snapped it shut.

I sent Knox a look as if to say, *what was that about Easton liking me?*

Knox just gave his head a small shake as Cillian led me to

a spot between him and Knox. That was probably safer than the spot that was open between Cáel and Easton. Easton might stab me with a butter knife.

Maddox's expression was carefully masked, but he studied me closely. "How's your head?"

I thought about it for a moment. "Not too bad."

"Any dizziness or blurry vision?" he pressed.

"I was just a little dizzy when I sat up this morning."

Maddox's jaw tightened. "You need to take it easy for a few weeks. Concussions aren't anything to mess with."

I nodded slowly. "Sure."

"Knox and Cáel will do all your packing," Cillian clipped.

I turned toward him. "Packing?"

"Yes. You'll be coming to stay here. I have a room being readied for you."

My spine stiffened, and Knox muttered a curse. "Excuse me?"

Cillian's green eyes darkened. "You heard me. We have people in our world who'd love nothing more than to harm you. We need to make sure you're safe."

"And what world is that, exactly?" I challenged.

Cillian's jaw worked back and forth. "It's complicated."

"Are you drug dealers? Or in a cult?"

His eyes flared. "You think we deal drugs?"

"What am I supposed to think? You have a ridiculous amount of money, you run some sort of underground club, and people want to kill you."

Cáel choked on something that wasn't quite a laugh. "She has a point. It wasn't a bad guess."

"I'd never help people put poison in their veins," Cillian snapped.

I met his angry stare. "So, a cult, then."

He let out a low growl. "We're not in a cult."

"Then why the hell did those people want you dead? Want *me* dead because I've been spending time with you?"

Cillian let out a long breath. "The Corbetts. They feel like we've encroached on their turf. They don't want anyone to see success other than themselves. They'd do anything to bring us down. And now that they know you're important to us…"

"They'll do anything to hurt me, too," I whispered.

He jerked his head in a nod. "We won't let that happen. It's why you're going to stay here."

I glared at Cillian. "Try *asking*."

Knox choked on a laugh and tried to hide it with a cough.

Cillian scowled at him and then turned that thunderous look to me. "Will you *please* stay here so that we can keep you safe?"

Who was I kidding? I'd be terrified to go back to the dorms alone, knowing that more of those men might be out there. "Okay. I'll stay."

The tension bled out of Cillian. "Thank you."

"Sure," I mumbled.

I'd just be locked in a house with two guys who'd made me come harder than I could've dreamed, one controlling alpha male I wanted to climb like a tree, my professor who could barely look at me, and my maybe-boyfriend's twin brother who'd rather stab me than smile at me. What could go wrong?

CHAPTER FORTY

Hayden

I watched Easton's back as he retreated from the dining room. He'd mumbled some excuse the moment he'd finished his breakfast. I let out a long breath, slumping against the chair.

Knox squeezed my knee under the table. "He'll come around."

I wasn't so sure about that but nodded anyway.

"Knox, Cáel, get Hayden to campus so that she can collect her things. I'm sending enforcers with you, as well," Cillian ordered, his voice low.

"Enforcers?" I squeaked. "That definitely sounds like some sort of gang."

Cillian let out a rumble of annoyance. "We're not in a gang or in the mafia, and we sure as hell don't sell drugs."

I just glared at him.

Cillian sighed, taking my hand and squeezing. "I'll explain everything once you're back, but you need to move quickly."

Memories from last night flashed in my brain. I definitely didn't want a repeat of that. Especially when I was alone on campus

I didn't say anything but tugged my hand from Cillian's and pushed back my chair. Knox and Cáel followed.

I cast a sidelong glance at Maddox, who hadn't said a word for the rest of breakfast. His eyes were locked on me, the amber burning brighter. The moment he caught me watching, he looked away.

I couldn't read him at all. There were times I thought he liked me, might even be attracted to me. But then there were others when I thought the most I could hope for was cool indifference.

"I've got my keys," Knox called.

Cáel wrapped an arm around me, tugging me to his side. "It's going to be okay, Little One."

"Easy for you to say," I grumbled.

Knox's X5 was pulled in front of the house, and he beeped the locks. "It's just going to take a little time."

Cáel held the door open to the back seat. I climbed in, and he followed.

Knox got in the front and scowled through the rearview mirror. "What am I? Your chauffeur?"

Cáel grinned at him, but it resembled more of a rabid hyena. "Want me to get you one of those little hats?"

"You try to put me in a hat, and I'll shave all those stupid fucking braids off your head," Knox shot back.

Cáel let out a low growl.

"Enough," I warned. "I've already got a headache."

Cáel turned to me immediately, kneading the back of my neck. "Want me to get you medicine before we leave?"

"No. I don't want to feel woozy. But a limit on the fighting would help."

Knox sent me a sheepish smile as he started the SUV. "Sorry."

"You should be. Plus, I like Cáel's hair."

I reached up, fingering one of the white-blond braids.

Cáel dipped his head, brushing his lips across mine. "I'm glad, Little One."

"No making out in the back seat," Knox grumbled. "It's not fair."

I couldn't help it. I laughed. It should've been weird, kissing Cáel while Knox looked on, but it felt as natural as breathing.

The ride to campus was quick, but I didn't miss the blacked-out SUV trailing behind us. Those enforcers Cillian had mentioned.

Knox pulled into an empty spot in front of my dorm, and the second SUV parked beside us. Cáel kept an arm protectively around me as we got out. Two hulking guys emerged from the other vehicle.

Knox nodded at them. "You can wait here. We'll be back in a few."

One lifted his chin in acknowledgment, but the other's jaw tightened. "I'm not sure that's a good idea—"

Knox cut him off with a hard stare. "It's broad daylight, in town. We'll be good."

The second man looked annoyed but held his tongue.

"Let's go," Cáel said, guiding me toward the dorm.

I pulled my key card out of my back pocket, swiping it over the lock. As we made our way through the dorm, students stopped to stare and whisper. I burrowed deeper into Cáel's embrace.

"Ignore them," he muttered. "They don't matter."

He'd gotten used to it, I realized. The rumors and whispers. I hated that for him.

In a matter of minutes, we made it to my dorm room door. I flashed my key card and poked my head in to make sure Delaney was decent.

The moment the door opened, her head jerked up from a textbook. "What the hell happened to you? Someone said they saw you leaving with Cillian and—"

Her words cut off as we stepped into the room, and she got sight of my companions.

"Cáel. Knox," she squeaked.

"Sorry I didn't call. It was kind of crazy."

Delaney shook herself out of her stupor. "Did you hear that three guys were *murdered*?"

"Uh, yeah." My body started to tremble as the memories hit me.

Cáel wrapped an arm around me, glaring at Delaney.

She gulped, taking a step back. "Hey, Knox. How are you?"

He tried to smile at her, but it came across as more of a grimace. "Good." He turned quickly to me. "You okay with me packing your closet?"

I nodded. "That's fine. There's a duffel at the bottom there. You can just put everything in that."

Delaney's brow furrowed. "What are you packing for?"

I worried my bottom lip. "I'm gonna stay with the guys for a bit."

Her jaw went slack. "You're moving *in* with them?"

Knox winced at her shrill tone as he hurried to put clothes in the bag.

"Just for a little while. I've been having a hard time sleeping and studying in the dorm, and they have extra space." Not entirely a lie.

Redness crept up Delaney's throat as she struggled for words. "You can't do that."

Cáel let out a low growl. "Of course, she can."

"What about your parents? They don't care that you're moving in with a bunch of guys?" she demanded.

I met Delaney's stare. "My parents are dead."

She flushed a deeper shade of red. "Well, I'm sure the university can't be crazy about this. There are rules."

I loved that she didn't say a thing about my parents. All Delaney cared about was the fact that I was going to be in close proximity to the guys she wanted for herself.

Knox dropped the bag with a loud thud. "Hayden's an adult. She's free to live wherever she wants. And we want her with us."

Delaney swallowed hard and then glared at me. "Well, don't

think you can just come back here. Once you're gone, you're gone. I could use a single anyway."

So much for a tenuous friendship.

"No problem," I mumbled, crossing to my desk to gather my books. I'd see about picking up extra shifts at the diner once all the craziness passed. There had to be a studio in town I could rent for cheap.

As I grabbed my bio textbook, I frowned. A ripped sheet of paper stuck out of the book. As I pulled it free, my blood ran cold as I took in the boxy scrawl.

THEY CAN'T HIDE YOU FOREVER.

CHAPTER FORTY-ONE

Hayden

 M Y HAND SHOOK, MY WHOLE BODY FOLLOWING THE action. Cáel and Knox were by my side in a flash.

"What is it?" Knox demanded.

I handed him the note.

He took it roughly, rage filling his eyes as he read. His gaze jerked to Cáel. "Call Cill. We need to move now."

Cáel nodded, pulling his phone from his pocket and hitting a few icons on the screen.

"What the hell is going on?" Delaney demanded.

"None of your business," Knox snarled. "It's not like you give a damn about anyone other than yourself."

Delaney gaped at him. "Knox, you don't understand. She's been an awful roommate. She's weird and—"

"Shut up," he snapped. "I don't want to hear another word out of your lying mouth."

Delaney gasped. "Knox," she whined.

He turned to me. "We need to move, Hayden. Get all your books, and let's go."

Cáel shoved his phone back into his pocket. "Reinforcements are on the way."

Knox jerked his head in a nod, gently pushing me to finish my packing. But all I could do was stare down at my desk. Someone who worked with those men had been in my room. They'd touched my things.

Nausea swept through me.

Cáel moved in behind me. "Breathe, Little One. Just breathe. One thing at a time."

"You've got to be kidding me," Delaney snapped. "Are you fucking both of them?"

I turned to look at my roommate. "Yes."

I wasn't. Not really. Not yet. But I was over Delaney's bullshit.

She paled. "You're lying. They wouldn't want…you. Not when they could have anyone on campus."

I snorted. "You mean not when they could have *you*. That's what's really going through your head, isn't it?"

Delaney straightened her spine. "You said it, not me."

Cáel just grunted something indiscernible.

"Keep holding on to hope," I muttered.

"Bitch," Delaney spat.

Knox moved toward her, but I placed a hand on his chest. "Don't. She's not worth it."

He just glared and started shoving books into my backpack.

A knock sounded on the door, and I jumped.

Cáel squeezed my shoulder and then crossed to open it. The two enforcers strode into the room, looking around as if they expected masked men to jump out at any moment. And maybe they would.

A shiver skated over my spine. How had they gotten in? The dorm was locked, as was our room. Apparently, they weren't men that locks kept out. I was suddenly more than glad that I'd be staying with the guys on their gated property.

One of the two enforcers picked up my duffel bag. The other reached out to take my backpack from Knox.

Cáel brushed his lips over my temple. "Do you need anything else?"

I shook my head. I really hadn't brought much with me to Ember Hollow. I hadn't had much to bring.

That thought had sadness sweeping through me. Not at the lack of physical belongings but at how small of a mark I made on the world. If I disappeared, would anyone even notice?

"It's going to be okay," Cáel whispered gruffly. "I promise."

I wanted to believe him. But I wasn't sure I could.

"Let's go," enforcer one said.

Knox nodded. "Hayden goes in the middle."

Cáel guided me to follow the enforcers while Knox brought up the rear.

"Don't you dare come back," Delaney yelled. "I'm getting the locks changed."

I'd sleep on a park bench before I went back to that dorm room.

I followed the massive men down the stairs and out into the quad. If I'd thought we'd gotten a lot of stares before, it was nothing to what we were getting now. Students didn't even try to hide it. They just halted what they were doing and gaped at us.

I didn't blame them. The four men around me were massive. And Knox and Cáel had larger-than-life reputations. But I didn't need the attention. I just ducked my head and moved toward Knox's SUV.

Cáel opened the back door and slid in behind me. Knox didn't make any chauffeur quips as he climbed behind the wheel.

In a matter of seconds, we were pulling out of the parking spot and heading back toward home. Except it wasn't my home, not really. I hadn't had one of those since I was eleven.

My eyes burned as pressure built behind them. Why was it now that I longed for that feeling of home? It wasn't like home automatically meant safety. What had happened to my parents proved that much. But maybe it gave the illusion of security. And I'd take even a glimmer of make-believe right now.

Knox drove at least ten miles over the speed limit, taking turns quickly and barely slowing at stop signs. The blacked-out SUV behind us did the same thing.

I breathed a sigh of relief as we hit the gravel road that I knew would take us to the guys' property. The tall redwoods towered over the road, giving an air of protection.

I forced myself to focus on the road ahead and nothing else. Not the note. Not that someone wanted to hurt me. Just the next few feet in front of me.

A large shadow danced across the road, and Knox cursed.

I frowned as Cáel took off his seat belt, leaning forward. "How many?"

"I don't know," Knox clipped back.

The shadow swept over the gravel again, almost as if a plane had passed between us and the sun.

I leaned forward to peek up at the sky, but there was nothing.

Then there was movement ahead. Something landed on the road. So large that it made our SUV shake.

I gaped, blinking rapidly. But no matter how many times I did, I couldn't clear my vision. Because in front of us was a massive creature. It almost looked like a supersized lizard. But it wasn't.

It was a dragon.

A roar tore through the air, and its mouth opened. And then flames were hurtling toward us.

Chapter Forty-Two

Hayden

THE FIRE WAS BEAUTIFUL. A MIXTURE OF REDS, oranges, and golds. But as it flew toward our vehicle, I knew it was as deadly as it was glorious.

Knox slammed on the brakes, and Cáel launched himself from the SUV. He opened his own mouth, and blue-silver fire shot from him. It formed a sort of wall or shield. The red-gold fire slammed into it but couldn't get through.

My breaths came in short, quick pants. This was all a dream. I was still unconscious from my attack last night. This was all in my mind. There was no other explanation.

"Stay in the car," Knox commanded. "Don't move until I or one of the guys come get you."

"You're leaving?" I squeaked.

He jerked his head in a nod. "I have to. If we don't shift, we'll be sitting ducks."

Knox didn't wait for me to answer. He was out of the SUV and launching himself into the air in a matter of seconds.

I sucked in a sharp breath, my vision wavering as he

transformed in front of my eyes. Gone was the man I was falling for, and in his place was a dragon, soaring into the sky. The creature taking flight was beautiful. A mixture of greens and golds. As I stared harder, I realized that its markings were a similar pattern to Knox's eyes.

"Because it's Knox," I mumbled. "Knox is a dragon."

I was hallucinating. That was the only explanation.

A dark green dragon swooped down, sending a blast of flames in Knox's direction. I couldn't help the scream that left my lips. But Knox ducked and rolled, avoiding the hit.

He returned a blast of his own, but his fire was pure gold. The shot hit the other dragon's wing, and it howled in pain, landing on the road ahead.

My gaze jumped to Cáel as he ran toward the beast. Mid-stride, he, too, transformed. His scales were white but also not. They were covered in a silvery shimmer but also seemed to change colors based on how the light hit him.

The two dragons ahead of us snarled, letting loose a torrent of flames.

My eyes burned as I watched Cáel narrowly avoid the blasts. But he quickly retaliated, catching one of the two attackers in the throat.

The sound that came from the falling dragon was inhuman and made my stomach twist violently.

Shadows danced in the sky, and I jerked my gaze upward. Half a dozen dragons filled the heavens. They seemed to be in battle, but I couldn't tell who was who, until I spotted another green-and-gold dragon. This one's markings were eerily similar to Easton's eyes.

He and Knox tag-teamed three other dragons, taking them out one at a time.

Tires screeched on the road ahead, and I saw Cillian and Maddox jump out of a sedan. The moment they did, more men spilled from the trees.

Panic gripped me. A trap. It was all a trap. To get all of them out here so that they could kill them one by one.

Movement caught my attention outside the SUV, but I breathed a sigh of relief as I saw the two enforcers circling. Protecting.

I swallowed hard as shadows emerged from the trees. More men. Too many.

My eyes burned.

This wasn't happening. I was dreaming. I had to be.

Cillian and Maddox fought with fire and blades, even hand to hand. They each took on four or five men, but I couldn't see how they'd be able to last.

The wind picked up, and Cáel let loose a vicious roar. Suddenly, snow was falling from the sky as he sent that silvery fire into the trees. Howls of agony reached the vehicle, and I knew he'd gotten several of the men attacking us.

The enforcers battled with their own attackers, trying to keep them away from the vehicle. My heart hammered against my ribs as I began searching the SUV for something, anything, that could help. I couldn't let them fight alone, not if I could help.

The only thing I found at first was an ice scraper. I didn't think that would do much of anything in terms of defense, so I threw it into the trunk and kept looking.

Feeling beneath the seat, my fingers closed around what felt like leather. I tugged it free. It was a black bag, similar to the one in the other SUV. Unzipping it, I pawed through the contents. Nothing seemed especially helpful until I came across a sealed bag with a metal instrument inside.

A scalpel.

I quickly peeled back the plastic and pulled it free. At least I knew this could do real harm.

A howl of pain had my head jerking up. Cáel had been hit by a blast of fire right in the shoulder. Maddox started toward him, not seeing a man sneaking up on his right.

I didn't think. I just launched myself from the vehicle, screaming Maddox's name as I ran toward him.

I didn't make it more than five strides before hands grabbed me by the hair, jerking me back against a hard chest.

"I heard there was a little dragon bitch, but I didn't believe it. Let's see how you scream."

CHAPTER FORTY-THREE

Maddox

THE WORLD SLOWED AROUND ME, MY BLOOD ROARING in my ears, as I saw the Corbett enforcer grab Hayden. Cillian shouted, and I saw another soldier out of the corner of my eye. He launched himself at me, but he was too slow. I pulled my blade, slicing him clean across the throat.

And then I was running. Toward Hayden. Toward my *mate*.

She'd risked herself to try to warn me. If something happened to her now, it would be all my fault.

We should've known the Corbetts would risk everything as soon as they knew of her existence. Should've known that they wouldn't wait to attack.

And now, it could cost us everything.

As I ran toward her, the enforcer's face came into view, and my blood ran cold. Jerome Corbett. He was one of their worst. Sick and deranged. I couldn't think about what he might do to Hayden if he escaped with her.

She screamed as he yanked hard on her hair, pressing a knife to her throat.

Jerome cackled, pressing the blade harder against her until a trickle of blood slipped free. "Such a beautiful scream. I can't wait to hear more."

"Stop, Jerome," I growled.

His gaze flashed to me, anger heating it. "If it isn't the professor. A day late and a dollar short, but what's new?"

I gritted my teeth. "Let her go."

Jerome just laughed harder. "Sorry, pal. It's not going to work that way. Dex wants her bred. Think of the new army we'll grow with all the babies she'll give us."

All the color drained from Hayden's face at his words.

Rage pulsed through me, my beast pressing at my skin, demanding to end this threat to our mate. "You know you'll never get away with her. We already have reinforcements heading this way."

Jerome glanced toward our territory, his jaw hardening. "Then we'll just have to end her altogether. Better than letting you abominations have her."

The blade slipped lower and sliced across Hayden's chest.

She screamed in pain, crimson blood staining her lavender sweater.

I charged, but Jerome jerked her back a step, bringing the blade to her neck again. "Ah ah ah. Don't move, Maddox. I might slip and get her jugular next time."

Hayden's breath came in quick pants, pain filling her expression, but her eyes locked with mine. There was so much trust there, hope and determination. Her gaze flicked down to her hand repeatedly, and that was when I saw it. A scalpel.

My focus jerked back to her face as she mouthed, *on three*.

Terror swept through me. It was too risky. But what other choice did we have?

Hayden licked her lips, mouthing again.

One.

Two.

Three.

She jerked her hand up and then slammed the scalpel into Jerome's thigh.

He howled in pain, his hold on the knife slipping.

I didn't wait, I flew. My dragon spurred the movement with his strength. My fist cracked into Jerome's temple, making him stumble to the ground. And then my blade sliced across his throat.

Jerome's eyes went wide as he tried to grab his neck, but it was too late. He was already gone.

Hayden stumbled and crumpled to the ground as the fight crested around us. War cries sounded from the sky, and I knew our backup had arrived. The moment they swooped down, the Corbetts began to run like the cowards they were.

I hauled Hayden into my arms, ripping her sweater. I needed to see how bad the injury was.

"I'm okay." Her words were barely audible, though. Whether that was from shock or injury, I didn't know.

The gash was deep and angry. It was bleeding like crazy. I stood, making for the SUV as Cillian ran toward us.

"What the hell happened?" he snarled.

"Jerome," I clipped, sliding us into the back seat. "We need to get her back to the house so that I can treat her properly."

But Cillian was already moving. He ran around to the driver's seat as the rest of our clan cleared the way in front of us.

I grabbed a gauze pad from the open medical bag and grimaced. "I'm so sorry, *Mo Ghràidh*. This is going to hurt."

"It's okay," she croaked.

I didn't wait. I pressed the trauma pad to her chest.

Hayden tried to stifle her cries, but she was only partially successful. Each sound was a slice to my skin, and I knew it was the same for Cillian. The steering wheel groaned under the force of his grip.

"You're going to be okay. I'm going to get you stitched up, and you'll be just fine." I was telling myself as much as I was telling her.

"I know," Hayden whispered. "I trust you."

She shouldn't, though. I'd failed to protect someone before. Failed to keep them safe.

Blood seeped through the pad, and I pressed harder, muttering a curse. "Hurry," I yelled at Cillian.

He pressed down on the accelerator.

Tears leaked from Hayden's eyes, and each one was a burn to my soul.

If she'd already shifted, an injury like this wouldn't be as dangerous. She'd just need to change to her animal form, and the wound would heal in minutes. But Hayden didn't have the first clue that she even was a dragon, let alone know how to answer the call of her beast.

Her breaths came in ragged pants, and her eyes started to close.

I pressed harder against her wound. "No, *Mo Ghràidh*. Don't close your eyes. Stay with me."

I couldn't lose her. Not her, too.

CHAPTER FORTY-FOUR

Hayden

P AIN FLARED WITH EACH BUMP OF THE SUV, BUT MADDOX didn't let go. His smoky, burnt-orange scent wrapped around me in a comforting embrace. I couldn't think about what I'd just seen, couldn't try to make sense of it. All I could do was breathe through the pain.

Cillian pulled his phone out of his pocket as he drove. "Get the caster to the main house, now."

A voice I didn't recognize came over the phone. "Already on the way."

Cillian hung up without another word, dropping the phone into the cupholder.

"Caster?" I whispered to Maddox, confused by the word. My voice was barely audible, and my vision wavered a bit.

I watched as Maddox battled against the rage bubbling inside him. He was usually the picture of control, but not now. "Someone who can help. They have healing abilities."

My eyes widened.

He kept the gauze pad pressed to my chest. "Don't worry, *Mo Ghràidh*. We're going to help you."

The gates to the property opened before we even neared, men and women with guns flanking it. My throat constricted as we flew past. What had I gotten myself into?

In a matter of minutes, we were pulling up to the house. Cillian jumped out of the driver's seat and came around to open the back passenger door. His normally deep green eyes darkened to almost black as he took me in. "Let's move."

Maddox lifted me from the vehicle, and I couldn't help the whimper of pain that escaped my lips.

"I'm so sorry, *Mo Ghràidh*. We're almost there." His voice was a hoarse whisper, agony and anger trying to break free.

Cillian jerked open the front door, leading us through a maze of hallways until we reached a room I'd never seen before. It was light and bright, some sort of sterile medical space.

Maddox lowered me to a bed, while Cillian was already moving around us, pulling various bottles and first aid items.

Footsteps thundered down the hallway, and the door flew open. Cáel was by my side in a flash, Knox hot on his heels.

Cáel pressed his forehead to mine, struggling to steady his breathing. "You're okay."

I tried to lift my hand to his face to comfort him, but the action hurt too much.

"Don't move," Knox ordered, his eyes wild. "Just hang on. East is getting help."

I frowned at that. But before I could question it, Easton stormed into the room, expression thunderous. His gaze jerked to me, zeroing in on my blood-soaked sweater. His face paled as he swallowed hard. "I've got the caster."

Easton stepped to the side to reveal a lanky guy who couldn't have been much older than me. His face was pale as his gaze jumped around the room.

Cillian strode toward him, his massive frame towering over the poor guy. "If you heal her, you'll have a safe haven for the rest of your days. If you hurt her, I'll rip you apart piece by piece."

"Cill," I croaked. "Don't."

The guy swallowed hard. "I can help her."

Cillian jerked his head in a nod, stepping out of the way so that the younger guy could pass.

He crossed to me, looking down and wincing. "I'm Marcus. Can I help you?"

"Hi," I got out. "I'm Hayden. Please."

Marcus nodded and then listed off a series of things, half of which I didn't even recognize. But the guys around me sprinted into action, bringing all sorts of items to a rolling table.

The only one who stayed was Maddox. It was as if he couldn't let go of my hand. And I was glad about it.

Marcus began mixing ingredients into a sort of paste, little lines appearing between his brows.

Cáel bent, his lips ghosting over my forehead. "I'm so sorry, Little One."

My gaze found his, so many questions in mine. But he didn't offer a single answer.

"Can someone cut her sweater off?" Marcus asked. "I need to apply the salve."

Knox moved quickly, grabbing medical scissors and cutting the beautiful cashmere now stained with my blood. As he peeled it away, I couldn't help but whimper.

"Do something for her pain," Cillian snapped.

Marcus glanced at him uneasily. "This will help. I just need to get it on."

He grabbed what almost looked like a paintbrush and began spreading the paste over my chest. I thought it would hurt, but the moment it touched my skin, I sighed in relief.

"It's helping," Knox whispered in wonder.

"Step back for a moment," Marcus instructed.

A series of growls filled the air.

"It will give her the best chance for complete recovery," he explained.

Reluctantly, the guys took a step back. Everyone except for Easton and Cillian, who were already keeping their distance.

Marcus began chanting in a language I didn't recognize. A green energy emanated from his hands as he held them over me.

My skin heated, and I swore I could feel my flesh knitting back together. A gasp escaped my lips as black smoke lifted from my body. Knox hurried to open a window, and the smoke lifted through it.

A tingling sensation spread through me like a wave, bringing with it energy and…peace? A second later, Marcus dropped his hands and stumbled backward.

Maddox caught him, offering him a stool to sit on.

"Thank you," Marcus mumbled.

Knox and Cáel were back by my side in a flash.

"How do you feel?" Knox pushed.

I blinked a few times, trying to survey my body. "I feel…great?"

I said it like a question because it shouldn't have been possible. There was no way.

Cáel dipped a cloth in a bowl of water, gently swiping it across my chest.

I gasped as I looked down. There was no wound. Just the faintest scar you could barely see.

"It's gone," I whispered.

Cillian crossed to Marcus, extending his hand. "You have my loyalty for life."

Marcus's eyes bugged. "Th-Thank you, Alpha."

"My enforcers will take you back to your cabin so that you can rest. I'd appreciate it if you could check on Hayden again later today."

Marcus nodded, getting to his feet. "Of course."

And then he hurried out of the room.

I pushed up on the bed, my gaze sweeping the space. "Will someone tell me what the hell is going on?"

A muscle in Cillian's cheek ticked. "We're dragon shifters. And you're one, too."

CHAPTER FORTY-FIVE

Hayden

MY BREATHS CAME QUICKER AS I STARED AT CILLIAN. Images of the dragons that had filled the sky swirled in my mind. Flashes of Knox transforming, then Cáel. Dragons. Dragon shifters. That was what Cillian had said.

"This isn't real," I whispered. "I'm dreaming."

Knox moved in front of me, crouching low and taking my hands. "It's real. I know it's a lot to take in—"

"A lot to take in?" I snapped. "You're telling me that you transform into some magical creature. I watched it happen, but I know it can't be real."

"And you will, too," Cillian said. His voice was perfectly even. That mask was back in place.

My breaths came quicker. "Stop it."

Knox squeezed my hands. "Dragon shifters have been around for centuries. We live in the shadows, along with other supernaturals."

My mind swirled. What other kinds of beings existed? I wasn't sure I wanted to know.

"Most of us live in groups called hordes or clans. It's like a chosen family."

I tried to focus on Knox, on his words. The idea of a chosen family was nice, but I still couldn't get past the transforming-in-to-a-mystical-creature bit.

"Is your family fighting?" I asked.

Knox's brow furrowed in confusion.

"She means the Corbetts," Maddox said as he washed my blood from his hands with a cloth. "They're a rival horde, not our family."

My eyes found Cillian. "Sounds like a gang to me."

He scowled. "We're not gangs."

"Okay, sounds like the mafia, then," I accused.

That muscle in his jaw fluttered wildly again. "We do what we have to—whatever it takes—to protect ourselves and the people we care about."

I bit the inside of my cheek. "And you can transform whenever you want?"

Cillian nodded.

"But today, people had to see freaking *dragons* in the sky."

Knox squeezed my hands again and pushed to stand, releasing me. "These forests are enchanted. We're free to be who we are. Humans won't see us in our dragon forms."

"But I saw you," I reasoned.

Cáel dropped a kiss on the top of my head. "You aren't human, Little One."

I shook my head vehemently. "I'm not a dragon. I've never transformed. My parents weren't dragons."

"That you know of," Cillian argued.

I slipped off the bed, pulling my cut-up sweater tighter around me. "You're wrong. It's not possible—"

"It is," Knox said gently. "If a dragon experiences trauma early in life, it can block the shift. You lost your parents so young, in a very traumatic way."

I swallowed the lump in my throat. "My parents would've told me."

"Female dragons are extremely rare," Knox explained. "It's why I was so shocked the day we met. Even more so when I realized you were our true mate."

"True mate?" My head swirled.

Cáel nodded. "These kinds of bonds are rare for our kind. But it's why we all feel so drawn to each other. The Universe has destined it."

Cillian watched me warily. "You will always have a choice, Little Flame. But know that we were made to love you."

My head thrummed in a staccato beat. "It's not possible. My mom would've told me." The protest was weak at best.

"Your parents could've been hiding you to protect you," Knox said, voice gentle. "They likely wanted you to have a normal life."

I sucked in a sharp breath as memories assailed me. *"Where is she?"* The stranger's words echoed in my mind.

Cillian moved then, striding into my space. "What do you remember?" he ordered.

My eyes filled with tears, and they spilled down my cheeks. "The man that killed my mother. He kept asking where *she* was. Were they looking for me?"

Cillian shared a look with the rest of the guys, and I had my answer. Nausea swept through me. Suddenly, my sweater felt heavy, sticky with my drying blood.

"I need a shower. Please. Can someone take me to a shower?" I begged.

Pain swept across Knox's expression. "Of course."

"She can use my room. It's closest," Cillian gritted out.

Knox pressed a hand to my back, guiding me out of the room and down the hallway. I didn't register anything at all as we walked. Not until we were in a black marble bathroom and Knox was turning on a massive shower.

He sent me a pained look. "Do you want me to help you?"

I shook my head. I didn't want anyone to touch me. I didn't want anyone to be close to me. I just wanted everyone and everything away.

Knox hovered for a moment. "Okay. Just call out if you need something."

I didn't say anything. I didn't nod. I just stood with my arms wrapped tightly around myself as I waited for him to leave.

The moment the bathroom door shut, I let my arms drop. I needed this sweater off, everything gone. I battled with the cashmere until it fell to the floor. I kicked off my shoes and pulled off my filthy jeans. I let my bra and underwear fall, too. Then I made a beeline for the shower.

The hot water scalded my skin, but I didn't change the temperature. I watched as the water swirled red around the drain. Then it faded to pink. And finally, it ran clear.

Only then did I move. I reached for the shampoo on the little shelf cut into the wall. Opening it, I sniffed. It smelled faintly of Cillian. That just made my chest ache.

Were they right? Was I their mate? My throat constricted at the thought.

I scrubbed my scalp with the shampoo and conditioner as my mind whirled. I felt drawn to all five of them. Attracted on a level that was more than sexual. Even to Easton.

My eyes burned as I rinsed the conditioner. How could this be real? None of it made any sense.

An image of my mother filled my mind. Her panicked face as she hid me away in the attic. Had she died because of me?

Pressure built in my chest. Pain swirled all around.

I forced myself to stay focused on the task at hand. Clean. I had to get clean.

I grabbed the bodywash and squirted some into my palm. Rubbing my hands together, I created a foam and spread it over my arms and then my chest. My fingers stilled on the faint scar.

Marcus had *healed* me. I'd been cut open, bleeding, and he'd used magic to stop it all.

I wanted to believe I was having some sort of psychotic break, but a small voice inside me told me that wasn't true. It told me that the guys were right. That they were dragons, and I was one, too.

The laugh bubbled out of me, harsh and hysterical. A dragon. A million questions swirled in my mind. None of which I had the answers for.

Shutting off the water, I stepped out of the shower and grabbed for a towel. I knew it must've been one of Cillian's, but I didn't care. I wrapped it around my body and found another for my hair.

Looking around the steamy space, I found my bloody clothes gone and a pile of fresh ones by the door. *Interfering dragons.*

I huffed out a breath as I changed into cozy sweats. I'd never felt anything this soft before and didn't want to even think about how much it had all cost. I towel-dried my hair the best I could but knew I'd be dealing with a rat's nest tomorrow.

Hanging the towels back in their place, I squared my shoulders and headed for the door. As I stepped out, I expected to find Knox but came up short when I saw Cillian sitting on his bed, his head in his hands.

Slowly, he looked up, his gaze sweeping over me. "Are you okay?"

"No," I answered honestly.

Pain streaked across his expression.

I crossed then, unable to see that agony and not do something about it.

The moment I was within reach, Cillian's arms encircled me, pulling me to him so that his face was pressed to my belly. He burrowed into me. "Scared a century off my life today."

A lump formed in my throat. "A century?"

Cillian rubbed his face back and forth across my belly. "Dragons live a long time."

"Good to know," I muttered.

Cillian straightened, tipping his head back, and his hands lifted to my face. "You're everything to me, Hayden. Nothing can happen to you."

I brushed my palm over his buzzed head, the hair tickling my skin. "I'm right here."

Our gazes locked, and my head lowered. My lips hovered just above his.

Cillian's eyes blazed then, sparks of bright green dancing in them. "Careful, Little Flame. You're not ready for me."

CHAPTER FORTY-SIX

Hayden

MY HEART HAMMERED AGAINST MY RIBS AS I WATCHED Cillian's eyes spark and swirl. The challenge was clear in his voice and in his words.

"Remind me I'm alive, Cillian."

All I wanted was to be in the here and now, to forget the earth-shattering information I'd learned just hours ago. To do nothing but *feel*.

Cillian's hand trailed down my neck. "My dragon will want to mark you."

I stilled. "Does that mean we're…mated?"

Cillian shook his head as his thumb stroked my pulse point. "The mate bite will have my dragon venom in it. It will leave a permanent sign on your body, just like you'll leave one on me."

Blood roared in my ears as some voice deep inside pushed me to bite Cillian, to tie myself to him for all eternity.

"My dragon knows you're not ready for that. But he still wants the world to know you're his."

I arched a brow at Cillian. "A bit barbaric, no?"

His lips twitched. "You can bite me right back."

My core tightened at his words. I wanted that. But why? I'd never felt that sort of urge before.

Shadows swirled in Cillian's eyes. "I'm not like my brothers. I need certain things…"

My brows pulled together as his thumb kept stroking.

"Complete control. Complete submission."

Unease flitted through me. "What does that look like?"

Cillian's hand dropped from my neck, and I missed it instantly. He leaned to the side, opening one of the drawers on his nightstand. He lifted something, extending it to me.

The black rope was perfectly coiled and tied. I reached out, running my fingers over the fibers. It was smooth as silk but somehow still held an ominous promise.

My gaze lifted to Cillian's face. His eyes were hooded now.

"Just watching you touch that rope has me hard as a rock," he growled.

I bit my bottom lip, heat pulsing low. "And you what? Want to tie me up or something?"

Green sparks danced across his eyes. "Yes."

"Why?"

Cillian's jaw tightened. "I need to feel in control. I crave your total and complete trust. Giving yourself to me to do whatever I want with you."

I studied his beautiful face, not missing the scattering of faint scars that dotted it. And I knew there was a story behind his need. A story he wasn't quite ready to give me. But if neither of us took the first step, we'd never make any real progress. And despite everything that had happened, I wanted that progress with Cillian, with all of them.

"Okay," I whispered.

Cillian's eyes flared. "Okay?"

I nodded.

"Little Flame…"

I lifted a finger to his lips. "Trust me to know myself. To know what I want. And what I need."

And right now, I needed Cillian. I needed to lose myself in him.

His jaw hardened to granite as if it were taking everything in him not to pounce. "You need to know your safe words."

I frowned. "Safe words?"

Cillian jerked his head in a nod. "Yellow means you're approaching a limit of what you can handle. Red means everything stops."

My stomach dipped and rolled. Would I need Cillian to stop?

"What slows us?" he pressed.

"Yellow," I whispered.

"What stops?"

"Red."

Cillian stroked my cheek. "Good girl."

More heat pooled, wetness gathering between my thighs, and he'd barely touched me.

My tongue darted out to wet my suddenly dry lips. Cillian's gaze zeroed in on the action.

"Step back," he ordered.

I swallowed and did as he instructed. But I hated the loss of him, his heat, his touch.

Cillian ghosted his thumb across his bottom lip. "Strip."

My core tightened, but I didn't wait. I lifted my sweatshirt and tee in one movement. Then I slid off the sweatpants. I stood there in nothing but a lacy bralette and cheeky boy shorts.

"So beautiful." Cillian stroked himself through his joggers, and I could see his length straining to get free. "Lose everything."

His voice held a grit that skated over my skin.

It was as if my body had no choice but to obey. I unfastened my bra, letting it fall. Then my fingers went to my panties, shimmying them free.

Cillian stood, strode toward me, then circled, taking me in. "Like a work of art."

A finger reached out, skating down my spine.

Every nerve ending in my body cried out for more.

"On the bed, Little Flame. Hands above your head."

A shiver coursed through me, but I obeyed, climbing onto the massive mattress and lifting my hands.

Cillian moved more quickly than I would've thought possible. He tied one wrist, then the other. Then he moved to my ankles. As he pulled the last knot taut, I tested my bindings. There would be no getting free.

Cillian's eyes flamed as he stared at me. "How do you feel?"

"Exposed and turned on."

He grinned, and for the first time, it completely lit up his face. "You're a masterpiece. Breasts thrust high. Pussy glistening already. You do like this, don't you, Little Flame?"

My core pulsed, and more wetness gathered, but with my legs spread wide, there was nowhere for it to go, and I knew Cillian could see it.

His nostrils flared. "Need something?"

My breaths came faster. "You."

Cillian growled, shucking his shirt and pants, his shoes already gone. "Tell me again."

"I need you."

Then he was on me. Cillian's face dove between my thighs, his tongue spearing deep.

My back arched as I cried out.

"You're like heaven and hell," he snarled as his tongue moved to my clit.

"Please," I begged.

"Need to come, Little Flame?"

"Yes," I breathed.

"Not until I'm inside you. I need to feel you shatter, need you to milk my cock until I'm wrung out."

Everything spasmed as he slid two fingers inside.

"Not yet," Cillian commanded, his tongue circling that bundle of nerves.

My thighs trembled, and I wasn't sure I could hold back my orgasm.

"Don't make me punish you." Cillian's hand struck out, his fingers slapping the inside of my thigh.

A moan slid free, and Cillian jerked back, his eyes blazing. "You liked that."

"Yes," I admitted, my hips shifting, wanting his fingers deeper.

"You're going to be so much fun to play with, Little Flame."

My inner walls tightened around Cillian's fingers, and he cursed, tugging them free. Then he was hovering over me. "Tell me you're ready."

"Please," I crooned.

Cillian didn't wait. He drove inside me on a vicious thrust. Tears leaked out of my eyes with the force of the sensation. But I only wanted more. More of him. Of this. Of us.

He thrust into me over and over. It was unlike anything I'd ever felt before. It was so much that dots of light danced in front of my vision, and my muscles shook.

Cillian roared, thrusting once more, impossibly deeper. His canines lengthened, and he sank his teeth into the juncture of my neck and shoulder.

The world around me shattered. I let loose a scream as my orgasm hit, but the pleasure was everywhere, from the tips of my toes to the ends of my hair. Cillian was everywhere. And as I took all he had to give, I knew my world had been forever changed.

Chapter Forty-Seven

Cillian

MY FINGERS STROKED UP AND DOWN HAYDEN'S SPINE. Her skin felt like liquid silk beneath my touch. She'd fallen asleep hard and slept through the day and night, but I hadn't closed my eyes for a second.

I couldn't stop touching her, couldn't stop watching the rise and fall of her chest. I needed to assure myself that she was here, still okay, breathing. That she hadn't befallen the same fate as my mother had.

Anger swirled deep, rage at what my mother had endured at my father's hands. I thought that ending his life would've brought me a modicum of peace. But it had only stirred up the nightmares.

Hayden mumbled something in her sleep, kicking out her legs. My lips twitched. My Little Flame was a violent sleeper. Even now, she was spread out like a starfish, face shoved into a pillow.

I kept up my ministrations, up and down.

Hayden let out a moan, rolling to her back and blinking up at me. "Hi."

I grinned down at her. "Hi."

Who the fuck was I now? Smiling and not knowing the English language?

I cleared my throat. "How are you feeling?"

Hayden's cheeks heated, and she bit her bottom lip. "Good."

My dick twitched the moment her teeth sank into that plump lip. I wanted to do the same, but I wanted to draw blood.

I reached out to trace the brand on Hayden's neck. My dragon was supremely pleased with himself about that one. It would last for a few weeks at least.

Hayden shivered. "Why does that feel so good?"

My smile only widened. "It's a link of sorts. Between you and me, to the pleasure we shared."

Her breaths came faster as her gaze dipped to my mouth.

"Don't look at me like that, Little Flame. I can't take you right now."

But, God, I wanted to. Wanted to drive into her so hard that I was imprinted on every inch of her body.

"Why not?"

The pout in her words had me chuckling. I cupped Hayden between her legs, keeping my touch gentle. "You have to be hurting."

The fresh flush to her cheeks told me I was right.

"It's not that bad," Hayden mumbled.

I brushed my mouth across hers. "Need to be gentle with you for a few days."

"Gentle sounds kind of boring after yesterday."

I tried to rein in my shit-eating grin. My girl liked to play. The fates had matched me with just who I needed. And now she was all mine. Ours.

Hayden's stomach rumbled, and she covered her face with her hands.

I kissed her temple. "Come on. We need to get you fed. You've slept for almost twenty hours."

She jerked upright at that. "I what?"

"You needed it."

"But I had a shift at the diner. My afternoon classes."

"Maddox made sure you were excused, and I got in touch with Fiona."

Hayden's shoulders relaxed a fraction, but she instantly slid out of bed, searching for her discarded clothes. "I need to make sure I get caught up. And Fiona must think I'm the biggest flake ever."

"She doesn't. She's a member of the horde, so she knows what happened."

Hayden stilled as she went to pull on her sweatshirt. "She's a dragon?"

I shook my head. "Wolf shifter. But she has sanctuary with us."

"Wolf shifter…" Hayden whispered. "What else is there?"

"Too many things to count," I said, sliding out of bed.

"I think I feel a headache coming on," Hayden muttered.

I dropped a kiss to her head. "You'll deal. It'll take some time to learn everything, but you'll make it through."

She let out a huff of air. "I hope you're right."

I grabbed a pair of boxer briefs from my drawer and tugged them on, then guided Hayden into my bathroom. I found her a toothbrush, and we set to work readying ourselves for the day.

It felt so incredibly *normal*. I never in a million years thought that was something I'd have. Getting ready with a partner in the morning, a *mate*. But there she was, blonde hair a tangled mess and eyes still a little bleary.

As Hayden rinsed the toothpaste, the wide neck of her sweatshirt revealed the bite mark along her collarbone. My dragon roared in pleasure. My human half knew she'd have to wear something that covered it, but my beast wanted the world to see.

She looked up at me, shifting uncomfortably. "Is it going to be weird that we, uh, you know? Will the others be mad?"

I wrapped my arms around Hayden, pulling her into me. "They may be jealous, but they'll also be happy. When one of us gets closer to you, we all feel it."

Hayden's eyes widened. "Really?"

I nodded. "I knew something had happened with you and Knox before he even fessed up."

She frowned. "But you were mad at him."

"I was. Because he was the reason you got sick. Sexual closeness tethers you to us in a way. When he kissed you, it made your body need physical touches from us. I knew you weren't ready for that, but Knox screwed it all to hell."

"This is crazy," she whispered.

I brushed my lips across her temple. "I tried to get us all to hold back, but when we killed for you, it was all over."

"Another kind of tether?"

I nodded. "A soul tether. We could break it if you wanted, but it would be painful for all parties involved."

Hayden looked up at me, her violet eyes shining. "I don't want you to break it."

Relief swept through me. "Good. Because I think it would kill me to walk away from you, Little Flame." Her stomach rumbled again, and I laughed. "Let's get you some food."

I hurried to dress in jeans and a Henley. I should've showered—my brothers would scent Hayden and sex all over me—but I couldn't. I needed her scent with me to calm me.

Once I was dressed, I took Hayden's hand and led her out into the hall toward the dining room. Voices sounded, and I knew we were the last to arrive. As we stepped inside, everyone stopped.

Cáel's lips twitched as he took us in. He stood, crossing to kiss Hayden quickly. "Morning."

"Morning," she mumbled, blushing that pretty pink.

He grabbed her hand and lifted it, exposing the faint marks from the rope. He glanced at me. "Have a good night, brother?"

Silverware clattered to a plate, and Maddox shoved back from the table and stormed out of the room.

Hayden paled. "I should go—"

I shook my head. "Let Mad get himself under control."

She pulled her hand free from my grasp. "No. I need to talk to him."

I tried to follow her, but Cáel placed a hand on my chest, stopping me.

"Let her go," he said. "She might be the only one who can get through his thick skull."

I glanced down the hallway, worry digging deep. Maddox was so lost in his martyrdom that I wasn't sure there was a force on this Earth that could bring him out.

CHAPTER FORTY-EIGHT

Hayden

I HURRIED DOWN THE HALLWAY, JUST CATCHING SIGHT OF Maddox as he stormed up the stairs. I jogged after him, my heart beating faster with each step. A door slammed up ahead. The sound vibrated through the air, hitting me in waves.

Slowing in front of the closed door, I bit the inside of my cheek. The message was loud and clear: *Do not enter*. But I took a deep breath and reached for the doorknob.

Opening the door, I stepped inside and had to fight my gasp. The bedroom was huge, and three of the four walls were floor-to-ceiling bookshelves. And they were jam-packed with books of all kinds.

My gaze swept over the spines. There was everything from thriller fiction to science textbooks. I wanted to pour over each one to try to learn more about Maddox.

"Go away, Hayden," he growled from his spot at a massive window. But he didn't bother to look at me. He simply stared out at the surrounding forests.

I didn't leave. I shut the door behind me and crossed toward him. "Talk to me."

A muscle in Maddox's cheek fluttered. "Don't feel much like talking."

"But you do feel like making a scene," I challenged. "If you really didn't want someone to come after you, you would've made some excuse about why you needed to leave breakfast rather than storming out."

Maddox's eyes flashed gold. "Maybe I didn't want to sit around while Cillian threw it in our faces that he'd fucked you six ways from Sunday. You think we can't smell it on him? On you?"

"Smell it?" I squeaked.

"We're half beast, Hayden. All our senses are heightened. Just like I can feel your panic right now."

Oh, hell. There'd be no hiding anything from these men.

I squared my shoulders, refusing to cower or let Maddox embarrass me. "From what you've shared, sex is a normal piece of this puzzle. Am I wrong?"

That muscle fluttered again. "Not with me, it won't be."

I studied him for a moment, looking and trying to truly see. "Because you're my professor?"

Maddox's gaze jerked back to the forest. "Yes."

I let the silence swirl between us for a moment. "You're lying."

His fingers balled into fists. "The university would fire me if they found out."

"I'm sure they would, but there's no reason for them to know. This is something else." I wasn't sure how I knew, but I was 100 percent certain. Maybe it was my strengthening bond with the guys, or maybe it was just that I'd been watching Maddox closely enough to know that he was hiding something now.

"I'm not made for a mate bond, Hayden."

His words ground into my chest, but I swallowed down the hurt. "Why not?"

Maddox's gaze flicked to me. "I don't trust myself."

I frowned at him. "To do what?"

"Protect you." The words were ripped from Maddox's throat as if he had to forcibly remove them. "Yesterday is just more proof of that."

I gaped at him. "You saved me."

"No. I almost got you killed." He ran a hand through his dark hair. "You think I don't know that you leapt out of that damned car to warn me? You put yourself at risk, and I couldn't get to you. Not in time."

Pain coursed through his voice, each word holding agony.

"But we got through it," I argued. "Together."

Maddox shook his head, beginning to pace. "That fucker held a knife to your throat. He cut you. *Twice.*"

I could still feel the bite of the blade against my skin, still feel the terror coursing through me. "I got away. I'm fine. There's barely a mark on me."

His jaw worked as he stalked back and forth across the room. "Not good enough. If these idiots had half a brain, they'd send you far away. Leave you with guards and out of our reach. Out of our ruin."

My heart jerked in my chest, and I swore I felt a roar of agony beneath my skin. "Good thing it's not up to you, then."

Maddox stilled, his gaze coming to me, fury pulsing there. "I had someone once."

Fresh pain swept through me, a different kind of torture. Because there was love and loss in Maddox's voice. Love and loss that didn't belong to me.

I shouldn't have been feeling the jealousy that pulsed through me. It didn't make sense. Not when I'd only known him for a matter of weeks. But it was there just the same.

"She trusted me. To protect her. To shield her," Maddox rasped.

My eyes burned. "What happened?"

"The Corbetts took her. They tortured her and left her broken body on the hood of my car."

I sucked in a breath. "Mad—"

"Don't," he clipped. "She wasn't my mate, but I cared for her."

"You loved her."

Maddox turned toward the window again. "I should've loved her. She gave me everything she had to give."

"It's not your fault."

He whirled, stalking toward me. "You don't understand. You didn't grow up in this world. It's bred into us, a biological need to protect our partner. I failed. Just like I failed again yesterday. You should run, *Mo Ghràidh*. Because I'll ruin you in every way possible."

Maddox stopped a mere inch from me. My ragged breaths made my breasts press against his torso, but I didn't move. "I'm not afraid."

"Now who's lying?" he challenged.

Heat swept through my skin, a mixture of anger and embarrassment. I moved without thinking, closing the distance and taking his mouth.

The moment his taste exploded on my tongue, I moaned.

The sound broke something in Maddox. He growled into my mouth, hauling me against him. His hardening dick pressed against my belly, only stoking the flames between us. He took and took, his hands digging into my ass as he pressed me harder against himself.

One hand grabbed my sweatshirt and tee, hauling them over my head. And then his mouth was back on mine. Maddox trailed kisses and nips down my throat.

I was so lost in the sensation that I didn't hear the door.

"Mad—oh, shit," Knox mumbled.

Maddox dropped me like I was a branding iron. I stumbled backward, almost falling on my ass.

His eyes were wild, jumping between me and Knox before finally settling on me. "This will never happen again. Stay the hell away from me."

And then he was gone, leaving me in nothing but my bra and sweats, staring after him.

CHAPTER FORTY-NINE

Hayden

I WAS QUIET ON THE RIDE TO CAMPUS. I SAT IN THE BACK SEAT of Easton's G-Wagon, staring out the window. I could feel Knox's periodic glances from the front seat and Cáel's worry from beside me. But I ignored them both. For once, I was grateful for Easton's cool indifference.

Maddox had made sure he got the distance he wanted. I hadn't seen him again. Knox had apologized over and over again, but it wasn't his fault. He'd gently helped me back into my sweatshirt and kissed me so tenderly, I'd almost started crying.

Even now, the pressure behind my eyes was brutal. But I wouldn't give in. I worried if I let myself break now, I'd never stop crying. There was too much swirling in my head. Dragons. An entire supernatural world. My parents. My *mates*.

My stomach twisted on that last thought. Two mates who wanted nothing to do with me. But fate, or whatever ruled the supernatural world, had chained them to me.

Guilt swirled. They shouldn't be forced into this.

Easton pulled into a parking spot in back of the science

building, two blacked-out SUVs taking the spots on either side of us. Cillian had insisted on eight guards accompanying us to campus, and Maddox had secured us all special passes to park in the faculty lot. No one thought the Corbetts would make a move right away, but they weren't taking any chances.

I grabbed my backpack and opened my door. Four enforcers waited. They were dressed casually, but they stuck out like a sore thumb. How they thought they were going to get away with following me everywhere, I had no idea.

Knox pulled me into a hug. "It's going to be okay. I promise."

But that wasn't a promise he could make. So, I didn't respond.

Easton cleared his throat. "We're going to be late to psych."

Knox reluctantly released me but not before brushing his lips across mine. "Text me if you need me." He glanced behind me at his brother. "Stick close. Cáel and I will meet you after class, and the enforcers will be patrolling the building."

"I know," Easton grumbled.

Cáel moved in, kissing me deeply. "Be safe, Little One."

What I wanted was to ask Cáel and Knox to hide me away somewhere I could forget all about the events of the past few days. But I wasn't about to let my scholarship go down the drain. "I will," I promised.

Cáel released me, and as I started toward the building, Easton fell into step next to me. He held the door open, and I stepped inside. Students milled around, finding their way to various classes.

"I'm sorry you're stuck with me."

Easton glanced over at me, frowning. "Someone needs to stay close."

"But it shouldn't have to be you."

That frown deepened, confusion marring his beautiful face.

"You don't even like me," I mumbled. "It shouldn't be your responsibility."

"I never said anything about not liking you."

My footsteps slowed, and I stared up at him. "I'm sorry, but calling me a piece of ass the first time we met pretty much implies as much."

Easton winced. "It's not about you," he muttered.

My shoulders slumped. That much might be true. But it almost hurt more. That who I was wasn't enough for Easton to get past whatever bullshit he had swirling in his head. Maybe none of this was about *me*. Maybe Knox, Cáel, and Cillian didn't like me for me either. Maybe I was just a *mate* to them. The thought made me sick to my stomach.

Movement caught my attention ahead as three girls leaned close to each other, whispering and stealing glances in our direction. Oh, hell. I tugged on my sweater, making sure it covered the mark along my collarbone, but I knew it did.

As we got closer, a few words caught on the air.

"Delaney said she's basically their whore. They're getting a kick out of the fact that she'll let them do *whatever* they want to her," one girl said.

Her friend leaned in closer. "It's sad, honestly. Can you imagine having that low self-esteem?"

The third girl just scoffed. "They've ruined her reputation for the rest of college. She'll have to transfer after they dump her."

Heat burned in my cheeks, and that pressure was back behind my eyes.

"Don't listen to them," Easton grumbled.

"It doesn't matter."

Nothing really did. Not anymore. Part of me wished I could turn back time and never come to Ember Hollow. But the moment the thought swept through my mind, I knew I didn't mean it. Even with everything I'd been through, I couldn't wish away Knox, Cáel, and Cillian.

I hurried into the lecture hall, finding an empty seat toward the back. Easton surprised me by taking the one next to me.

A guy in front of us turned around, grinning. "Dude, when you're done with her, I wouldn't mind taking her for a ride."

Easton was out of his seat in a flash, throwing the guy to the floor and pressing his forearm to his throat. "If you even look at her again, I'll break every bone in your body. You'll be pissing out a tube and eating through one, too."

"Shit, man. I'm sorry. I-I didn't know," he wheezed.

"Well, now you do." Easton gave one more hard press against the guy's throat and then stood, dusting himself off.

Students whispered loudly and pulled out cell phones. I knew it would be a matter of minutes before the gossip had made the rounds.

"Everyone in your seats," Professor Brent said, walking into the room. He scanned the space, his gaze settling on me. He scowled as Easton took the seat next to me.

"We'll begin where we left off," Brent continued.

I did my best to focus on his voice and the slides behind him. I took the best notes I'd ever taken in my life. But I could feel Easton glance at me every so often. His gaze had a unique feel to it. Heat but with a bite, like minuscule spikes dancing across my skin. Prickly, just like the man himself.

Before long, the bell rang, and I gathered my belongings. Easton waited for me. Like a silent sentry, he followed me down the lecture hall's stairs.

Brent looked up from his papers. "Hayden," he clipped.

The urge to groan was so strong. I didn't have it in me to deal with my advisor today, too. But I stopped anyway. "Hello, Professor."

He scowled at me. "I heard you've missed several classes."

I gulped. "I was feeling under the weather again. But I've made up all the work and talked to all my teachers."

Brent's jaw worked back and forth. "I expect more from you. We'll meet tomorrow at five p.m. to discuss these recent issues."

It was no longer a request but a requirement.

I winced but nodded. "Okay."

Brent's gaze lifted to Easton, who hovered behind me, and his eyes narrowed, but he didn't say a word.

Easton let out a low growl as we walked away. "I don't like him."

"You and me both," I mumbled.

The moment I was outside, I was hauled into strong arms. Cáel nuzzled my neck, breathing deeply. "Are you okay?"

"Fine," I lied.

Cáel just held me tighter.

"That guy still breathing?" Knox asked his twin.

"Unfortunately," Easton answered.

Knox shook his head. "Hopefully, your message was heard loud and clear."

I burrowed deeper into Cáel's hold. "You can't just beat everyone to a pulp who says something mean to me."

Cáel held me tighter, scowling. "Why not?"

"We can't let it slide," Knox said. "It'll only get worse. We give a show of strength now, and it'll be better in the long run."

I sighed. "So much for being normal."

Knox's brows pulled together in confusion.

"All I wanted for my college experience," I explained. "Just to be normal. I'd always been the foster kid, the one with the dead parents. People look at you differently. I thought I finally had a chance to blend in, to have a normal college experience."

Knox moved into my space, his hands framing my face. "Hayden."

"It's dumb."

"No, it's not. If you want normal, we can give you normal," he vowed.

Cáel scoffed, keeping his hold on me. "We wouldn't know normal if it bit us in the ass."

I should've listened to Cáel.

CHAPTER FIFTY

Hayden

MY LAST CLASS OF THE DAY WAS A FRESHMAN ENGLISH seminar. I didn't mind it, even if some of the literary analysis seemed like grasping at straws to me. Because it was a freshman class, none of the guys were in it with me. They'd assured me that enforcers would be just outside if anything were to happen, but it meant that my classmates were free to make their opinions of me known.

"Slut," one said as she tried to disguise it with a cough.

I ignored her, packing up my bag.

My lab partner from bio was in this class, too, and she sent the girl a glare, moving closer to me. Her dark hair swung in front of her face like a shield, but I could still make out the scar marring her cheek. "Are you okay?" she whispered.

I saw the tremble in her hands and knew it had taken everything in her to just ask the simple question.

I did my best to give her a genuine smile but knew it fell short. "I'm okay. People are idiots."

She glanced at the mean girl two rows back. "People are the worst."

I slung my backpack over my shoulder. "Some of the ones here definitely are."

Wren shoved her hands into her pockets. "I hope they leave you alone soon."

Before I could say another word, Wren hurried toward the classroom door. I frowned at her. She was possibly the first genuine person I'd met at Evergreen, other than my guys.

"Have fun sucking dick for room and board," a guy spat as he walked by me.

I let out a sigh. And Wren might be the last genuine person I met here, too.

The moment I stepped out of the classroom, I was flanked by two enforcers. One wore a scowl, but the other gave me a kind smile. "Ready to head home, Hayden?"

I nodded. "What's your name?"

"Pete," he answered with a grin. "And this is Terry."

"Nice to meet you both. Thanks for taking me…back." It felt wrong to say *home* when I knew Easton and Maddox didn't want me there.

"Of course. We'll get you home safely," Pete assured me.

We got a few sidelong glances and whispers as the two of them escorted me out of the building. I could only imagine what the rumors would be tomorrow. And all thanks to Delaney. I wouldn't wish her harm, per se. But I would wish her a lifetime of stepping on Legos in bare feet.

When we made it to the parking lot, two more guards joined our group. And while Easton's G-Wagon was gone, the two blacked-out SUVs were still present.

Terry moved to the back door of one and held it open for me. I scooted into the center seat while he and another enforcer flanked me. Pete and a fourth guard got into the front.

The ride home was silent, and I was thankful that no one tried to make conversation. I was exhausted. All I wanted was a long shower and to climb into a bed, alone.

Pete pulled to a stop in front of the gorgeous home, one I never thought I'd call my own, even in my wildest dreams. But I also never would've had a clue how many strings came with it.

The enforcers piled out of the vehicle, and I followed.

Pete inclined his head toward the house. "Go on in. We'll be patrolling the premises."

I nodded. "Thank you."

When I stepped inside, the silence swirled around me, and I realized I didn't have the first idea of where to go. The feeling of being out of place surged, and pressure built behind my eyes.

I stood in the entryway for a long moment, just staring at nothing, before a voice broke into my thoughts.

"Hayden," Knox called.

I looked up to find him, and he grinned down at me.

"Come upstairs. I have something to show you."

Fatigue swept through me, but I had no reason not to go with him. I trudged up the stairs until I reached the third floor.

Worry spread over Knox's expression. "Rough day?"

"Not all sunshine and rainbows," I admitted.

He wrapped an arm around me and pressed a kiss to my temple. "Well, hopefully, this boosts your mood."

Knox guided me down a hall. I caught tiny snippets of Cillian's and Cáel's voices from up ahead. I'd never been on this floor before. It had the same lush carpeting as the second floor and gorgeous art on the walls.

Knox slowed, gently pushing me through an open door. "We wanted you to have a place that felt like yours."

I stilled as I stepped into the bedroom. It was massive, and the scent of fresh paint still clung to the walls. Walls that had been made a lavender gray. There were massive windows that looked out onto the forests behind the house, a sitting area with bookshelves, a desk for studying, and a bed that looked like three king-sized ones rolled into a single mattress.

An abstract painting hung above the bed, made of circles and lines. Taking it in, my eyes burned. "Are those atoms?"

Knox shrugged. "You love science."

I turned to face him, Cáel, and Cillian. It was then I saw that they were all in scrubby clothes, splattered with paint. Lavender paint. "You gave me a room."

Cáel attempted a grin, even though it came across as more of a grimace.

"You painted my room," I said, my voice trembling.

"We wanted you to feel at home," Cillian said, worry creasing his face.

The tears came then, fast and hot.

"She's crying," Cáel accused, panic lighting his voice. "Why is she crying?"

"I think because she likes it," Knox said softly.

"I love it." I only cried harder.

Cillian strode toward me, lifting me into his arms. I clung to him like a spider monkey as I sobbed.

"Th-thank you."

"Ssshhhh, Little Flame," he crooned. "Everything's okay."

It was far from it, but I let Cillian lie to me.

Cáel moved in on one side of me. "We can paint it another color if you don't like this."

A laugh bubbled up through my tears. "I love this color."

He frowned down at me. "I don't like it when you cry."

"Sorry, big guy. Sometimes my emotions just leak out of my eyeballs."

Knox chuckled as he kissed my hair. "We want you to feel at home and have some normalcy."

I released my hold on Cillian, letting my feet drop to the floor. "I hate to break it to you, but a massive room in a mansion isn't exactly normal."

Knox grinned. "All right, our kind of normal. And there's more."

I let out a shuddered breath. "I'm not sure if I can take any more."

"Just one more thing," Knox promised. "There are some clothes in the closet. Pick out a sexy-ass dress and be ready by nine p.m. We're taking you out."

I glanced around at the three of them. "All of you?"

Cillian gave me a shark grin. "All of us."

Holy hell…

CHAPTER FIFTY-ONE

Hayden

I STEPPED BACK, TAKING IN MY REFLECTION IN THE FULL-
length mirror. I bit my bottom lip. Maybe this had been a
mistake.

The closet surrounding me was full to bursting with new
clothes. The tags had names like Valentino and Balmain. Brands
that I knew cost more than I'd make at the diner in a year.

But I did my best to ignore that fact. Instead, I'd focused on
getting ready. I'd soaked in the huge bathtub for over an hour,
shaving everything meticulously and scrubbing my skin until it
was smooth as silk. I'd put a mask in my hair and then blow-dried
it perfectly, adding a few waves for volume.

Not only had my new closet been bursting, but my bathroom was, too. It had every skin and hair care product under
the sun and more makeup than I'd ever know what to do with.
I'd taken my time with that, rimming my eyes in a purple so
dark it was almost black, but it made my violet eyes burn bright.
I'd coated my lips in some sort of gloss that made them look
plumper, too.

TWILIGHT OF EMBERS

But I worried I'd taken a wrong turn with the dress. Knox had said sexy. This was definitely that.

I took in the Balmain number and couldn't help but laugh. It was a silk slip dress, short with the most delicate straps. The combination meant I couldn't wear a bra and could only wear the tiniest pair of underwear I'd ever seen. But it was the design on the fabric that had me giggling.

Painted in pastels, with lots of silvers and lavenders, was an old-school angel painting. Like those you'd see in an Italian museum. It seemed only fitting to tease heaven when these guys teased me with devilish temptations.

Bending, I slid my feet into black stiletto sandals with chunky buckles. I felt stylish and sexy, not exactly *normal* like Knox had promised, but so much better.

I grabbed a silver clutch with my phone, ID, and cash, and headed for the door just as the clock struck nine.

Voices sounded from down below. I could make out each of them. Cillian, Knox, Cáel. Each had its own unique cadence and tenor. I tried not to let disappointment flare at the absence of Easton and Maddox.

I shoved it down, focusing on the promise of a night out with three guys who meant the world to me. As I reached the landing, all talking ceased. The three men stared up at me, gaping.

The shock and heat in their eyes had my confidence surging. And they looked delicious. Cillian wore his signature black suit, dark green eyes swirling with need. Knox wore dark slacks that fit him perfectly and a button-down shirt with the sleeves rolled up, exposing tanned and muscular forearms, and an expensive-looking watch. Cáel was completely himself in dark, ripped jeans, motorcycle boots, and a leather jacket that was artfully distressed.

"Hi," I whispered.

Cillian was on me in a flash, his hands skimming down my sides. "Little Flame…"

"An angel who will drag you right to hell," Knox muttered as his hand grazed my ass.

My cheeks heated as I looked up at Cáel.

He let out a low growl. "I think we should stay home."

I couldn't help but laugh. "I worked way too hard on my makeup to stay home."

Cillian's arm looped around me. "She's a work of art. Our girl needs to be admired."

My nipples pebbled under his gaze, straining against the fabric.

He grunted. "This dress is going to kill me."

"But what a way to go," Knox muttered, opening the front door and holding it for us.

As we stepped outside, it was to find a sleek limousine waiting. I grinned at Cillian. "Seriously?"

He shrugged. "Usually, I like things a little more low-key. But we're pulling out all the stops."

"You think that racecar you drive is low-key?" I challenged.

Cáel choked on a laugh. "She has a point, Cill."

"Get in the damn limo," Cillian griped.

Sliding into the vehicle was a bit of a challenge with how short my dress was, and I didn't miss the guys staring intently at my legs. I bit my bottom lip to keep from laughing.

Cillian tugged it free as the driver pulled away from the house. "You're full of mischief, Little Flame."

"Never," I vowed, laughter in my voice.

Knox caught my leg, lifting it onto his lap and stroking my skin. "Wouldn't want you any other way."

His fingers teased and toyed as we drove, never venturing too high but driving me out of my mind just the same.

When we pulled to a stop, I blinked a few times. "The club?"

Cillian studied me for a moment. "We're going to a

different part of it. Will you be okay? I don't want to bring back bad memories."

I shook my head. "It's fine."

"We have double the security now, and you have your own personal guard," Cillian assured me.

I grabbed his hand, squeezing. "I know I'm safe with you."

His eyes glowed that deep green. "Good."

Getting out of the limo, Cillian extended his hand to me, helping me out. I smoothed my dress down and took in the back entrance. There was no flash, but there were two huge guards standing by the door.

"Alpha," one greeted, ducking his head.

The other simply dipped his chin as he opened the door.

Cillian led me inside, Knox and Cáel following behind us. The space we stepped into was completely different from the front area of the club. The patrons were as varied as you could imagine, from what looked like bikers to bankers, but they all held an otherworldly beauty.

Knox moved in on my other side. "This part of the club is only for supernaturals."

"Oh," I breathed, looking at everyone with new eyes, wondering what they might be.

The music here was quieter, more sultry. Booths were lined in maroon leather, and tables were made of black marble.

"Like it?" Cillian asked.

I could tell from his voice that he truly wanted to know.

"It's beautiful," I admitted. "Definitely more my speed than the cage dancers."

Cáel chuckled, coming up behind me to whisper in my ear. "Wouldn't mind seeing you dancing in a cage. For us only, of course."

My skin heated at the promise in his words.

"Let's get you a drink," Cillian purred, leading me to the bar.

A man in a sharp suit dipped his head. "Alpha, what can I get for you?"

Cillian glanced at me. "Hayden?"

I swallowed, licking my lips. "Club soda with a splash of pineapple juice?"

The bartender nodded and took everyone else's drink orders, as well. A man flagged down Cillian, and he was pulled away, but Cáel quickly flanked my other side as we sipped our drinks.

He and Knox kept finding ways to touch me, innocent brushes of their fingers that made me feel anything but. I pressed my thighs together, trying to alleviate some of the throbbing there.

"I think we should take her downstairs," Knox rasped.

Cáel's eyes flared. "Little intense for her first time here, don't you think?"

I looked back and forth between the two of them. "What's downstairs?"

Knox grinned. "A different sort of playground."

"What the fuck are you thinking?" Easton snapped as he stepped up to our group.

Any amusement slipped from Knox's face. "What's your problem, East? You said you didn't want to come. Fine. But don't try to sour our good time."

The pain of those words landed. Easton had been invited, but he'd refused any proper time with me. I shouldn't have been surprised, but it still somehow managed to sting.

Easton's jaw worked back and forth. "I didn't know you were coming *here*. I just stopped in to get a drink."

But as I took him in, I knew it was more. You didn't come to a bar alone without an ulterior motive. One like picking up a woman that wasn't me.

I straightened my spine. "Let's go downstairs. The energy's too stuffy up here."

Easton's eyes flashed gold. "You're not ready for that."

I glared at him. "You wouldn't have the first idea about what I am or am not ready for. Because you haven't taken a single second to actually get to know me. I'd say that you should, but I know you're too much of a coward to try."

And with that, I stalked toward an elevator, hoping it was the one that would take me down to whatever waited below. Even if it was hell itself, it would be a heck of a lot better than Easton's vitriol.

CHAPTER FIFTY-TWO

Hayden

I CAME UP SHORT AS I TOOK IN THE TWO HULKING MEN NEXT to the elevator bank. They stared down at me, their faces impassive masks. I swallowed hard. My storming-off exit would lose its effect if I couldn't actually make it to whatever was downstairs.

Heat flared at my back as an arm came around me. Pine and rain filled my nose as Knox pulled me close.

"It's okay, Harrison. You can call the elevator."

One of the guard's eyebrows raised the barest amount in question as he pressed the button.

"Cill's gonna fry your ass," Cáel muttered.

"Let me worry about him," Knox shot back.

"Trust me, I'm not going to get between the two of you when he loses it."

What the hell was in the basement that would set Cillian off like Cáel was warning?

The elevator dinged, and the doors opened, revealing plush leather walls. Knox guided me inside. Cáel following. The moment the doors closed, Cáel turned to face me. "If you want to leave at any time, just say the word."

I stared up at him, trying to read his expression. There were only hints of emotion playing beneath the careful mask. Worry. Agitation. Heat.

Mere seconds passed before the doors were opening again. Different music filtered over us. I wasn't exactly sure how to describe it. Low and sultry, it pulled at you.

Cáel turned, stepping off the elevator. He led the way to what almost looked like a hostess stand. But the woman running her gaze over Cáel and Knox looked like anything but someone who might lead us to a restaurant table. She had raven hair and bright red lips. She wore a leather dress that was cinched so tightly, it had to make it hard to breathe.

"Evening, boys," she purred as she opened what almost looked like a cigar box. "What color tonight?" She pulled a red silk band from the box, handing it to Cáel. "Always red for you. But one day, I'm going to get you to change your mind."

Cáel simply grunted in response, fastening the colored silk around his thick wrist.

"Red, please," Knox said, dropping his hand from my waist.

The woman's eyes flared and then shifted to me. She frowned slightly. "Interesting. And you?"

"She'll have red, as well," Knox answered for me.

Annoyance flitted across her perfectly made-up eyes. "I guess the rumors are true."

"They are," Knox said coolly. "Feel free to spread the word."

The woman's jaw tightened, but she nodded. "Enjoy your evening."

"Oh, we will," Knox said, a grin in his voice.

"What do the bracelets mean?" I hissed.

"That you're taken or don't want to be touched," Cáel informed me as we made our way deeper into the space.

It was darker than the bar upstairs. The lights had a purplish hue to them. It fit with the hypnotic music pumping through the speakers.

A woman in front of me turned to the side, and I gasped. The dress she wore was made entirely of delicate chains, but there was nothing underneath. You could see everything from her nipples to the small dusting of hair between her legs.

But it was more. A leather band was cinched around her throat and attached to a chain that a man held in his hand. A collar and leash?

Heat flushed my body as I watched her follow him through the crowd. Where the hell was I?

Cáel leaned down, his lips skimming my ear. "Supernaturals are incredibly sexual beings, shifters especially. We crave touch, contact."

My gaze flitted up to his, questioning. Cáel rarely let anyone but me touch him. Did that mean his animal half was starved for connection?

I lifted a hand, placing it on his stubbled cheek and stroking. He dropped his head to mine. "Little One," he whispered hoarsely.

Cáel brushed his lips against mine and then pulled back, his eyes hooded with promise.

I forced my gaze away from his, trying to take in my surroundings. My focus settled on a stage, and I stilled.

There was a woman restrained on what almost looked like some sort of medical bed, except the leather was too nice to be found in any doctor's office. She wore nothing at all, her red hair cascading over her shoulder and almost skimming the floor. Her arms were fastened to rests in the front, her legs to rests in the back. Her backside was on display as a man behind her brought down something against her ass.

I jerked as she cried out. But the woman's sound wasn't pain-filled, exactly. It was more.

"It's a sex club." The words didn't sound like they'd come out of my own mouth.

"Cillian wasn't big on calling it that," Knox said as his fingers ghosted over my belly through my silk dress.

The woman on the stage cried out again as the leather strands of whatever the man held in his hand came down hard across the globe of her ass.

"It's called a flogger," Knox explained.

My gaze jerked up to his face. "Do you do...this?"

He grinned. "I'm not really one for public play."

My stomach flipped; a mixture of apprehension and excitement flew through me. But the heat won out, pulling me closer to the stage, Cáel and Knox at my sides.

A second man stepped forward, lifting the woman's chin. She sucked his thumb deep into her mouth, and he groaned. The sounds and sights had my core tightening.

The first man brought the flogger down again, and the woman's thighs trembled as she moaned. The man soothed the sting of the swat with his palm, his hand dipping between her thighs.

Heat flared at my back, and smoky cedar swirled around me. "You like to watch, Little Flame."

It wasn't a question, but heat still licked my cheeks. I tried to look up at Cillian, but he gripped my chin lightly, forcing it back toward the stage. "Eyes on them. Don't look anywhere else."

My heart hammered against my chest, and I could feel Cáel's and Knox's gazes on me. The three of them were surrounding me, their heat, their scents.

Cillian's hand dipped beneath my short silk dress. "Yes?" he growled.

"Yes," I breathed.

His fingers tangled in my tiny thong, and a second later, he was shoving the fabric into his pocket. "To mark the memory."

My breaths came quicker as Cillian's fingers were back, teasing and toying.

"Keep watching," he ordered.

It was all I could do to focus on the three people on stage. The second man rounded the woman, unzipping his pants and stroking himself. He nodded at the first man. Number one brought the flogger down hard on the woman's ass, and number two slammed inside her.

She cried out, but there was no pain in her voice, only pure pleasure. Number two thrust into her over and over as the flogger whipped across her backside. My own core spasmed as her muscles shook.

Cillian growled in my ear as he slid three fingers inside me.

Knox moved in closer on one side of me, gazing down, eyes blazing gold. "So beautiful with those flushed cheeks, just begging for Cillian to make you come."

My walls tightened around Cillian's fingers, and I let out a whimper.

Cáel reached up, palming my breast through the silk of my dress. My nipples hardened to sharp points as my legs trembled. His fingers elongated one and then twisted as Knox nipped my ear.

It was all it took. I shattered. I would've hit the floor if Cillian's arm hadn't come around me. He held me upright as he extended the orgasm, pulling wave after wave of pleasure from me.

I struggled to catch my breath as I slowly came back to myself. Cillian pulled his fingers from my body, lifting them to his mouth and sucking them clean.

I gaped up at him, but he just grinned.

A figure bumped into Knox. And familiar green-and-gold eyes seared into me. A muscle in Easton's jaw ticked wildly as he glared down at me.

"Do me a favor and fuck her elsewhere next time," Easton growled. "I'd still like to have a little fun left in my life."

CHAPTER FIFTY-THREE

Hayden

I PUSHED OFF CILLIAN'S CHEST AND GAVE EASTON A HARD shove. "I'm not stopping you from doing whatever the hell you want. You want to grab some random and fuck her up on that stage? Have at it."

The gold in Easton's green eyes sparked and swirled. "Just knowing you were here would kill my hard-on before I had the chance."

I made an exaggerated show of looking at his crotch. There was something long and thick pressing against his zipper. "Something makes me think you're a damned liar."

A wave of rage hit me as Easton's hands balled into fists. "Just because the fucking fates chained me to you, doesn't mean I'll give in. My body might react to you, but you'll never steal my soul."

"East," Knox growled in warning.

But Easton just shook off his brother. "I still have my free will the last time I checked, and I don't want a damned thing to do with you. So just go use one of these assholes as your own personal vibrator. But remember, none of them actually chose you either."

Easton's words slammed into me, leveling blow after blow, each one worse than before.

My eyes burned, and my throat constricted, but I refused to let him see me cry. I didn't say a word, just took off running for what looked like a back hallway.

There was a scuffle behind me, and I glanced back in time to see Knox's fist connect with Easton's cheek. I didn't wait for them to sort it out. I dodged club goers and staff alike, moving deeper into the club until I spotted a hallway that read *Staff Only*.

I ducked down it until I reached an end that said *Exit*. Praying I wouldn't set off an alarm, I pushed the door open and stepped outside.

The cold air wrapped around me, but I welcomed the bite. Anything to distract me from Easton's brutal words. Words that I was terrified were true.

I stepped out farther, taking the steps that would bring me back to street level. The alley was blissfully quiet. Only the faint strains of music flared when a door opened around the corner.

I lowered myself to a curb and let my head fall to my knees. No matter how hard I tried to keep them back, a few tears escaped and coated my skin. I was sure my makeup had melted into a hot mess by now. But what did it matter? It was all playing pretend anyway.

Pretending that I could fit in this world. Pretending the guys had actually picked me. Pretending this could work.

It was all a joke. My chest constricted. Maybe I could transfer to another school, somewhere there weren't dragons or wolves or any other supernatural creatures. Somewhere I could just blend into the background. Hell, maybe I could just opt for online school and stay locked in a tiny apartment somewhere.

Footsteps sounded on the pavement, and my head snapped up as my body tensed. It didn't relax when Easton came into view. His man bun was slightly askew, telling me he'd been running. And his eye was already swelling.

But he still managed to glare at me. "What the hell are you doing out here?"

Rage flared to life somewhere deep, and I shoved to my feet. "Pick a fucking lane, Easton! You want me as far away as possible, or do you want me to stay inside like a good little girl?"

His chest rose and fell in ragged pants. "How about just not being a fucking moron? You were almost killed two days ago."

"I'm really sorry I wasn't. Then your life would be a hell of a lot easier, wouldn't it?"

Easton stumbled back a step as if I'd struck him. "Hayden—"

"Shut up. I don't want to hear any more. The push and pull is driving me insane. One second you hate me, the next I think we might be friends, and then you're telling me that nobody wants me here. Well, fine. I don't want to be around you either. Give me a few weeks to find a transfer or see if I can switch to on-line classes. Then I'll be out of your hair."

"Hayden—"

"No. Just no," I said, my shoulders slumping.

A tsking sound came from the darkness, and Easton whirled.

A man with reddish-brown hair stepped out of the shad-ows. "Doesn't sound like you've been treating our *bana-phri-onnsa* very well, Easton. Didn't your mother teach you better?"

Easton braced, taking up a defensive position. "Stupid move, Hal. You know you aren't welcome here. We're fully within our rights to kill you."

The man just grinned. "But I wanted to meet the illusive Hayden." His gaze skimmed over my body, making me shudder. "Even more beautiful in person. She'll be quite the prize."

"Over my dead body," Easton growled.

"That can be arranged." Hal's mouth opened, and it was as if everything happened in slow motion. Gold fire shot out, hurtling toward Easton.

I didn't think. I simply moved. I threw myself at Easton, knocking him out of the way. But I wasn't quite quick enough.

Fire collided with my chest in a brutal blow. The agony was instant, taking me to my knees.

Easton clambered to his knees, shock and horror on his face.

He tried to reach out to me, but it was too late. The fire was already consuming me.

Hayden's story continues in *Midnight of Ashes.*

Also by Tessa Hale

The Dragons of Ember Hollow

Twilight of Embers

Midnight of Ashes

Dawn of Flames

Supernaturals of Castle Academy

Legacy of Shadows

Anchor of Secrets

Destiny of Ashes

Royals of Kingwood Academy

The Lost Elemental

The Last Aether

The Queen of Quintessence

The Shifting Fate Series

Spark of Fate

Mark of Stars

Bond of Destiny

CONNECT WITH TESSA

You can find Tessa at various places on the internet.
These are her favorites…

Website
www.tessahale.com

Newsletter
www.tessahale.com/newsletter

Facebook Page
bit.ly/TessaHaleFB

Facebook Reader Group
bit.ly/TessaHaleBookHangout

Instagram
www.instagram.com/tessahalewrites

Goodreads
bit.ly/TessaHaleGR

BookBub
www.bookbub.com/authors/tessa-hale

Amazon
bit.ly/TessaHaleAmazon

ABOUT TESSA HALE

Author of love stories with magic, usually with more than one love interest. Constant daydreamer.